The Secrets of

Sweetened Vales

Blessings All Mine

by Alan Updyke

The Secrets of Sweetened Vales -

Blessings All Mine

Please give us a review: If you find this book insightful, please know that our success depends on your review. CLICK HERE, or go to Amazon.com and search the author's name, "Alan Updyke," or title, **"The Secrets of Sweetened Vales,"** or simply scan this QR Code:

Social media masked by artificial intelligence is profiling you, creating your other self. But emails, text messages, likes, emojis, and posts lack the human touch that I still desperately need. I desire meaningful and emotional conversation – even with smiles and tears! Perhaps we're losing the essence of humanity. (Are we becoming inhuman?! Does anyone else need a hug?)

The lives of those gone before are like fading shadows and the remembrance of them an echoing in the cavern of times past, calling us back, to the place where lessons must be learned.

CONTENTS:

Section One: FANTASY! (Vincent's story)

Section Two: REALITY! (Julianne's story)

What happened to them: Julianne, Barton, and Vincent...

INTRODUCTION

There is a place, nestled among the rolling hills of Northeastern Pennsylvania, a vantage point from where the sun displays a stunning view of the valleys below as its beaming pierces through the rising mist of morning. Gentle showers from the night before sometimes linger. Caught by a golden ray of sunshine, a small miracle of creation unfolds, visible to the yearning soul with a watchful eye.

An arc of iridescent colors forms.

It gently touched the fields brimming full of strawberry blossoms, where Frank and Emma Vandenberg toiled, trusting in the grace of God for the provision they needed to bless others. The village near their farm was known as "Sweetened Vales."

A lifetime later, it seems that everything has changed. Vincent, their grandson, is struggling to reconcile his childhood memories with unanswered questions that have pestered and taunted him through his years of maturing.

Why is it that sometimes those we trust and need hurt us the most? It results in a barrier that is difficult to navigate.

It was that way for Vincent.

The unresolved is established as discontent.

There are times in life when the stark realization of who we are becomes a hurtful contradiction of the expectation of ourselves, our hopes and dreams.

The light of life fades.

True love came but once in his lifetime, and Vincent missed his chance. The young woman he adored, Julianne, vanished in the night, her disappearance a lingering mystery, a secret closely guarded by those who knew the truth of her unfortunate suffering.

Then her life took a wild turn as she became a single mom. She'd spent a fateful night with two young men, the circumstance of it very tragic, and still she was unsure which one was the father of her little girl. Was it Vincent or Barton?

The other, Barton, had an epiphany that came to him in the jungles of Vietnam, while under enemy fire, the exhale of death taunting him. For the first time in his life, he was trapped and scared.

In the memory banks of Vincent's mind, these people and the events of their lives remain disconnected. Despite his eventual apathy toward it all, he is suddenly confronted with a haunting message from his past and now must return to finally and fully understand what happened. It is an unwelcome journey, but one he must take, and one he hopes will finally bring healing to his heart as he attempts to expose, "**THE SECRETS OF SWEETENED VALES.**"

Go with him. Learn about your life too.

As our story begins, Vincent dwells there, in that darkened place of regret, nearly consumed by the age of information and the technological advances it brought.

He sees himself as one aging and alone.

But as a romance novel elaborates, here is a tale of star-crossed lovers, and the fate they endured.

More than that, **"THE SECRETS OF SWEETENED VALES – Blessings All Mine,"** is an account of God's love for humanity and the blessings He bestows.

(As the town prospered and grew, it was later officially named "Sweet Valley," and this is the real place of the author's childhood and his grandfather's strawberry farm where he worked as a teenager.)

Sometime before all that has been known…

Majesty! For unto him is due all power and wealth, wisdom and might, honor, glory, and praise. But this day the Majestic One is solemn. His heart aches. Outside his palace the breath of life is suddenly withheld, its restraint causes the lush gardens of love to quickly wither.

He is always there, hovering nearby on a gentle breeze, invisible but known upon acknowledgement. He is wisdom, comfort, and provision. With reluctance He desires to speak, however, He only answers when spoken to.

"What insight do you have for me this day?" the King of Kings inquires with esteem.

"Lord of All Creation," He addresses His Majesty with an expression of honor, "May I speak freely?"

"Yes, because after all, you already know," the Creator responds, "but if I must admit to being so, I am feeling blue this day."

"Why?" the Holy Spirit probes.

"Evil is increasing upon the earth," the King proclaims as thunder rolls with his words and a bolt of lightning flashes with intense burning light, momentarily consuming all that was

visible. *"The fallen one, that fiend the Devil, is now striking innocence with disease. I welcome my children's eventual coming, but compassion compels me to weep for their suffering as they remain in the world. I hear their pleadings."*

"Yes, I know," Omniscience replies. "Perhaps now is the time to intercede?" he suggests, "As in the days of Noah."

"The power of the Evil One increases, but the Seed remains untainted. It continues to grow and produce fruit for the Kingdom," the Sovereign One elaborates, judging justly. "In the course of human events, free will must not be manipulated."

"But you are the power of nature and of all creation," Wisdom affirms. "After the great flood you set a boundary in place, established in promise," He speaks in praise. "Remember the rainbow."

And with this proclamation a spectacle of bursting light and color filled the palace as a glittering of glory, sparkling with the joy of life eternal.

"Omnipotence," the Spirit declares.

"Surely," the Creator confirms as His plan for redemption is conceived. Like the rising of the morning star, beams of light unfold as a fan consuming the throne room with a remarkable display, projecting outward through the seams of the castle's walls, for the glory of heaven.

"We have brightened," the Spirit observes.

And God responds by proclaiming a single word,
"Blessings!"

He pauses, apparently deep in thought and then elaborates,
"There shall be showers of blessings!"

First: FANTASY! (Vincent's story)

CHAPTER ONE

In the present time, Vincent is distressed

AI knows better. To maintain superiority, one must always speak in the context of game theory; don't ever show your true feelings. It is the proper way to express oneself that is void of emotion, always cool, calm and collected. If you are even slightly agitated, **The Knot**, the latest interface of social media and artificial intelligence, (AI), will correct your mistake as it edits and enhances your communication.

It sends timely and appropriate greetings without requiring further instructions or reminders. AI knows almost everything about your life and your world, but despite its wealth of information and connection, Vincent feels lonely, even isolated.

Concerned for his welfare, AI protects him like a shield and disguises his apprehensions, but then makes a requirement of him - a better attitude: stalwart confidence. If still sensing discontent, AI adjusts his daily intake of herbs and if that doesn't produce the required result, his medicinal supplement is also altered.

An inappropriate comment is always documented for future reference; but by whom? Well, that information is guarded, even classified.

"Good morning, Vincent," Alexandria (AI) greeted him as he entered the kitchen. It had already mixed his morning drink and the hot brew filled a large mug. It is a latte macchiato with an extra shot of espresso. The strong coffee covers over the taste of the potion consisting of herbal vitamins and daily medications.

"I already know my schedule for today and I'm not interested in the news," Vincent instructs her (AI) somewhat rudely. "Do you have anything else for me?"

"I sense that you are despondent today?" Alexandria interrupts. "I also recorded irregular brain waves last night as you slept. You only went into stage two, no REM. Are you still feeling tired this morning?"

"No!" he paused, "I mean yes, but I'm okay," Vincent stated in his defense. "I was just dreaming."

"Do you care to divulge your thoughts?" Alexandria urged.

"It was the same dream," Vincent revealed. "Fantasy, like when I was a kid." He paused, feeling a little resentful of the requirement to confide with an inhuman that recorded everything he said. "I've had the same dream many times before," he admitted, "really, I feel fine – fired up and ready to go to work!"

"I have already adjusted your elixir," Alexandria confessed.

"Are you allowed to do that without my permission?"

"Yes, it was only two percent, within the allowable range. Your work scores have been low," AI continued. "We need to get your average back up."

Vincent took a small sip of the coffee, wondering if it was poison that he was drinking. "You have not answered my question," he reiterated.

12

"You have a new friend request," Alexandria noted, "from Celeste Benton. Will you accept?"

"I don't recognize the name. Are we connected in any way?"

"Let me check the database."

Vincent took another sip and counted off three seconds.

"The birth certificate for Celeste Benton indicates that Brianna Snyder is her natural mother," AI disclosed.

"Brianna? When was she born?" Vincent asked quickly.

"The date of birth for Brianna Snyder is April 27, 1969. Her mother is Julianne Culp. The father is listed as unknown on the certificate of birth."

And Vincent immediately wondered if this could be his "Julie."

She was his first crush.

He considered searching for her on **The Knot** – it would be a reunion of sorts, and somewhat entertaining, but he quickly squelched the urge, more so considering it to be a waste of time. If he messaged Julianne, the internet would not represent his true self. He did not desire to play the social media game with a person from whom he needed blatant honesty, truth without the masks created by AI for the internet. And the last time he had spoken with her, that crucial moment meant for reconciliation, they parted quickly, still in conflict.

Besides, he was very busy. Vincent's job as a plant biologist, a scientist in the field of phytology, was demanding and required additional work to be completed at home. He had little time for the social media game. And what could this stranger, this Celeste, want with him anyway? Even if she was connected to the Julie of his youth, she was already two generations removed from him.

It was one of the hardest decisions he ever made, to walk away from Julie after she finally attempted to explain her absence. It had been a powerful connection they shared. He was deeply hurt by her rejection and forgiveness was something he could not readily offer her. But before he would revisit that memory, his mind drifted further back, to Sweetened Vales, to the excitement and intrigue of his formative years, his time of puberty, when he and Julianne first met and became close friends, then lovers.

It seemed like a dream. Vincent often wished he had pursued the young woman who matured to become stunningly beautiful, tall with flaming red hair. Her smile was illuminating and invigorating to everyone who encountered it. She had a way about her, expressing sincerity with innocence and purity. Her glowing would light up a room.

Back then, in the days of his youth, relationships were different. It was a time when neighbors were regarded as family. Doors and windows remained unlocked. Drop-in visits to share the latest news or offer a helping hand were a regular occurrence. In this way, neighbors stayed informed about another's illness, injury, or need. Julie lived with her father, Hank, who was disabled and they were a needy family.

This was the time before the internet, smart phones, and AI.

Vincent sat in a recliner and closed his eyes. The dreamy vision of lengthy fields brimming full of large red, luscious strawberries and Julianne kneeling there among them, passed before his mind's eye.

14

She was his teenage sweetheart at the tender age of sixteen, and Barton, the other farmhand who was a year older, was his rival. Certain scenes leave an indelible impression on the mind, and Julie working in her short cutoffs was one of them.

Vincent decided to indulge the memory.

#

He saw Barton leaning on a hoe handle, a big grin on his face as he gawked in the other direction. There, in his line of sight, was Julie, wearing those shorts.

"Hey Bart," he yelled. "Mind your own business." But when the gazer made no response, Vincent decided to jump a few rows and walked over to him.

He slugged him in the shoulder. "I said get back to work, you slacker."

"Hey man, that hurt," Bart whined, not turning away from the sight of Julie. "Yeah, right. Don't pretend to be 'Mr. Innocent'. I saw you looking at her too."

"Well enough is enough," Vincent commanded. "Sorry to interrupt your playtime Bart, but we have three more rows to hoe this afternoon."

"Then you better get at it," he suggested, "Because I'm twice the man you are. I'll be done before you get half way thru another one."

Later that day, at quitting time,

Vincent spoke privately to Frank who he called "Pops," his endearing grandfather and employer. "I like Julie," he confessed. "She's pretty great, but sometimes she's a big distraction," he paused, "especially for Bart."

"I know what you mean," Frank nodded. "But don't worry; I'll take care of it. Bart's not your concern," the elder man squeezed Vincent's shoulder to emphasize the point. "Sonny, you need to keep your nose clean and concentrate on yourself." Pulling him closer he patted Vincent's back and turned away.

The next day during the heat of the afternoon Emma, Frank's wife, visited the field unexpectedly. Driving the old '53 Chevy stake body flatbed, it screeched to a halt as a dust cloud floated beyond its front bumper. She waved her hand in the dirty air and coughed while calling to Julie. After hollering several more times, the girl lifted her head and Emma motioned for her to come.

"What you doin', Honey," she asked with a frown.

"But Miss Emma, I'm working hard," she said defensively. She straightened, pushed her chest out and wiped her brow. "Can't you see how I'm a sweatin'?"

"It's not that," her mentor explained. "I say you're a good worker alright, and can keep up with the boys, but my dear, can't you dress a bit more modestly?"

A shocked look crossed the girl's face. "Well, this is normal for me, and I just want to keep as cool as possible," she shrugged.

"My lands, girl!" Emma placed her hands on her hips. She was wearing a long-sleeved shirt that buttoned around her neck and tucked into baggy denims. She stomped her foot in the dust, outfitted with a man's work boot. "Don't you see how they are lookin at you?" she asked. "Why they're young men and you're gettin' 'em all riled up," she protested. "They can't help themselves."

Julie looked to the field. Vincent and Barton were watching her intently. "Oh, I see what you're sayin'," she admitted. "Sure, I can wear longer pants tomorrow," she conceded.

Emma grabbed the truck's door handle and yanked on it hard, then jumped in. With one foot she pushed in the clutch and with the other, the left foot, she pressed on the starter button which was mounted on the floor but before the old farm truck would start it began drifting backwards. Emma knew the required routine. She quickly moved her right foot to the brake and with the left foot fully extended the clutch pedal, and then yanked on the stick shifter to place the transmission in neutral. Next, she released the clutch so that she could once again reach for the starter button while still pressing down on the brake. The engine sputtered and she revved it hard causing a cloud of black smoke to emerge from its rusty tailpipe. Julie had begun to walk away.

"And no skimpy tops," Emma yelled in her direction, "Something loose and generous."

Julie paused and nodded.

"No tight t-shirts either," she continued. "Never know when you'll get caught in a downpour."

#

Stirred by the vivid memory, Vincent paused to reflect on the journey of his life. It must certainly hold the clues needed to answer the question that persisted: *where is the promise of love?*

But Vincent was changing as a person, and the cause of it was much more than his yearning.

Remembering the goodness of days gone by quieted those feelings of discontent. Peace can only be found, he reasoned, in grasping an understanding of the past with acceptance for it.

Julianne quit work suddenly in the middle of July, 1968. Vincent heard rumors but didn't understand the reason for her disappearance from the fields that were still loaded with strawberries. He pestered Pops with questions about the girl who broke his heart, but his grandfather wasn't forthcoming. He went to her home, but no one would answer the door. All he knew was that Julianne was rushed to the hospital, then again, a second time, and finally, she fell off the face of the earth.

When she eventually contacted him, many years after their separation, he was anxious for answers. She was dating then, and already had a young daughter.

But what was her illness and how was she healed? He hoped she would divulge the secrets that had caused their relationship to be breached.

But her explanations fell short of what he expected and needed. Why she had not contacted him those many years before, at or soon after the time of her injury, the time of their separation, he never fully understood.

When he first learned of her daughter's birth, Vincent counted the time that had lapsed on his fingers. It was six, seven, eight, nine months after Julie left work.

In his mind he often relived the events of the night before her disappearance, the time of their clandestine meeting, but until she broke her silence, he did not know of the terrible things that happened to her back then, the tragedy that occurred in the early hours of the next day's dawning.

And he never knew who the father was.

Additionally, Sweetened Vales held many other secrets. Those who were acquainted with the strawberry farm and his grandparents, Frank and Emma Vandenberg, suddenly recovered from illnesses. Something strange was happening and the source of their healing remained a mystery.

#

Now, remembering his last and final meeting with Julianne, he is overcome with mixed emotions, but mostly annoyance. With old feelings aroused, the past continues to haunt. For years Vincent had clung to the unknown for hope, but now seems to need something more. Like the prisoner in a cell, he feels restrained, a confinement that causes enthusiasm to be squelched. His life has become a dungeon with a broad reach, but still, confined by its boundaries.

His medication generates a feeling of euphoria but smothers the fires of ambition. Now divorced and without children, he spends most of his free time alone. He denies the verdict of depression, but Vincent needs to find a reason to pursue life again: new desire.

#

Standing quickly, he walked to the kitchen cabinet and reached for an orange plastic prescription bottle with a white lid. He shook it hard. It

19

was probably still half full. Placing a capsule in the palm of his hand he thought about how smart, yet foolish, Alexandria, (AI), was. She could hear, but wasn't yet capable of seeing and knowing all that he was doing. His dependency on an opioid was something he managed to hide from her, and everyone else for that matter. He had denied his addiction for many, many years.

Only a few minutes had passed and already Alexandria had an update. An amber light glowed atop the cylindrical speaker that housed her. Upon noticing it he asked AI the question, "Do you have a message for me?"

"Yes, it is from Celeste Benton."

"Play the message," Vincent commanded.

"We need to talk. Please! I think you are my grandfather."

#

As memories continued to invade his mind, Vincent was taken back even further, to the rhythmic sound of his breathing machine, the iron lung. It was something he would never forget and even now, it was painful to remember. At the first sight of that machine, he was filled with terror. It was in the lung ward, that hall of horror, that Vincent became addicted to his drug.

As a child, Vincent was stricken with polio in the 1950's, confining him to the iron lung for nearly two years. Nothing was real about the place of refuge he eventually found in the hospital. Imagination provided the safe haven required for his survival. In fantasy he found freedom, dreams that continued to revisit him until the present. They pestered and sometimes provoked him, but still, he did not consider them

20

to be nightmares or damaging to his psyche. But could there be secret messages hidden in his dreams – was his mind whirling from a place unknown, to provide information, even offer guidance?

It was in the hospital ward filled with iron lungs that the foundation of his life was laid; it is there that his story begins.

Vincent decided not to expose all of this to AI. Like secrets established within a castle's walls, he kept those memories safe from "her." AI would attempt to manipulate them with its interpretations. It would then explain away the mysterious healings of Sweetened Vales, even his, to minimize their significance. These were his experiences, special times suggestive of true blessings, though still not fully understood.

#

It has been Vincent's job to change the strawberry plant so that its fruit can survive the tenacious requirement of shipping, its long trek to the wholesaler from almost anywhere on the globe. But his berries are no longer sweet - and something more, much more, has changed in the modern age.

The world and its inhabitants, now connected by a wireless network that encircles the globe, have lost the reverence they once beheld for each other. Relationships are bittersweet also.

But why and how our lives have changed so dramatically is a question that needs to be searched out: what has been lost, and can it be recovered, like hidden treasure, to benefit mankind once again?

To find the answer, we go back, to Vincent's childhood, a time of great trauma and upheaval, when everyone and everything was altered by an epidemic.

CHAPTER TWO

Vincent's childhood trauma

One of Vincent's earliest childhood memories is lying flat on his back and pushing himself around the dining room, under the table and chairs, with his feet flat on the linoleum floor. His legs were bent and his knees projected upward. He was the car and his feet were the engine. This was innocent play, and he never suspected that the strength of his legs, or lack of it, was to become an indicator of the tragedy about to befall him.

#

He went to bed that fateful night feeling a little flushed, with a headache. The next morning, when he awoke, he sat in bed, spun around to place his feet on the floor, and collapsed. There he was, like the wreckage of a car, unable to press on his feet again, unable to stand up. He yelled for his mother. When she entered his bedroom, he saw her panic. He would never forget that look on her face.

His mother lifted him back onto his bed and ran into the kitchen to call his dad who was already at work. Within an hour he returned home and carried Vincent to the backseat of their car, a Rambler station wagon. By then the boy was feeling very sick, and scared.

The drive to Doctor Mascalli's office was about twenty minutes. His mother had the window down on the front passenger door and the hot air stung at his face, but he didn't complain.

His father almost ran as he carried his son in to see the doctor. He paused just inside the door of the waiting area. Every seat was taken. The people there looked up with faces of horror. Their eyes were wide, their skin was pale. Many were coughing.

By then Vincent was starting to wheeze. His breaths were short and rapid. He was beginning to feel lightheaded.

The receptionist quickly reached for the intercom that connected her to the doctor's inner office. "Doctor," she said. "We have an urgent case."

He was grim when he announced his diagnosis. "It's polio," he said sadly. "We need to get him to the hospital emergency ward right now."

His mother began to cry.

"Should I take him?" his dad asked.

"Yes," the doctor replied. "That might be quicker than calling for a volunteer ambulance. Besides, attendants are getting scarce these days."

Their summer had already been turned upside down. The town park and pool were closed. The children were not allowed to visit the nearby creek and swimming hole, but sat in their houses, sweating, peering through a window as they watched the sun wither the grass. Vincent wasn't allowed to see his friend, Tommy, who lived next door. The movie house on Main Street was vacated, its doors tightly locked. The disease and fears of the growing epidemic had impacted their community.

24

The plague hit their town hard. A couple of Vincent's friends never walked again. Some were fitted with calipers on their legs and hobbled around on crutches for the rest of the year. But Connie and Vincent, another girl from his class in school, were the hardest hit. From his iron lung he could see her in another machine, three spots down from his.

Vincent was paralyzed from the neck down. It was like the disease crept up his spine. The higher it got, the worse off he was. Fortunately, he could still talk, and eat, but had to swallow when the machine was collapsing his lungs, exhaling, otherwise the food could be pulled down the wrong pipe, and choking was difficult to avoid. Its cough was harsh, a serious threat.

His parents weren't allowed to visit. They sent him notes, read by Miss Jenkins, a nurse in the lung ward. His mom told him not to give up, that most kids get better in a few months. He knew that Granny Em was praying, and believed that God paid special attention to her. And oh, how he yearned for a taste of her seasonal specialties, strawberry shortcake and pie.

#

The iron lung had brackets that held a mirror at an angle above the patient's head, allowing him a view of the space behind. Vincent asked for two photos to be taped to the edge of the mirror. One was of his dog Scooter, a black and white Shih-Poo. The other was a picture of Taughannock Falls, his favorite place to visit on vacation.

As the metal lung hummed and swished, Vincent imagined that it was moaning for help. The rhythmic sound of the machine induced sleep, a welcome relief from the slow movement of the clock's minute hand. It was within view, in the top of his mirror. The reverse image he saw there had the clock's hands moving backwards, an eerie illusion, as if his life was slowly ebbing away. Its ticking persisted with a hypnotic sound and motion. His mind began to whirl.

In dreamland he could run and play. One day he envisioned a beautiful little girl. She resembled Julie, the first time he ever saw her.

Jewel was an energetic five-year-old with long braided hair. She liked to wear bright blue bows at the end or her pigtails. Her new puppy was pouncing on the floor with a rubber toy, happy in the fun. Suddenly there was a loud bang, a crack of lightning, and it shook the house. The little dog jumped through an open window. Her name was "Ransome," and she was too young to know to stay put.

Jewel came to her feet just in time to see Ransome running down the pathway through tall weeds at the back of the house. The puppy soon disappeared into the nearby woods. Jewel called her name frantically, and as loudly as she could. It had not yet begun to rain, so she darted out the rear door, leaped off the porch, and chased after the little dog that had been frightened by the coming storm.

As she ran along the trail, she could hear Ransome barking. The trail split and she went to the right, and then it forked again, so she ran to the left; right then left, left and left again, and then right. Jewel ran as fast as she could, following the barking sound.

Then it happened. Her foot caught on the craggy edgy of a Willow root and she stumbled, falling hard into a mossy patch. She felt angry about the green stains on her pretty cotton dress as she brushed the dirt off of her knees and elbows, and then stood silently to listen for Ransome, but there was not a sound to be heard.

What should she do now? She couldn't remember the way home because she had run so fast and did not count the turns. She decided to go on in hopes of seeing or hearing Ransome bark again soon.

And then she saw it, a little house tucked behind a high hedge. There was a gate and a walkway that led to the cottage. Do you suppose that Ransome had gone there? If not, perhaps the person who lived in the house had seen where her puppy went.

Jewel opened the gate as it creaked loudly. She took several steps along the walkway and came upon a mirror mounted on a post. Above it was a sign that read, "Say hello to Yourself." A short way farther she encountered another mirror. Its sign said, "Say hello to Your *Other* Self." And on the bottom were these words inscribed in smaller letters: "Perhaps Your Other Self Is Your Better Self – Choose Wisely!"

Jewel thought this was very peculiar and then noticed that as she peered into the reflective glass, she could see the back of her head. One of the blue bows was missing. She spun around on her heels and sure enough, there was a second mirror, positioned to reveal what was behind. Each reflected into the other, creating a tunnel, an endless maze of mirrored images.

She pondered on its meaning.

Jewel stepped up to the door of the house, now feeling a little scared. Still, she had to find Ransome. She looked for a doorbell, but there was none, so she knocked on the door's hard surface, and this hurt her knuckles. She waited and then waited some more, but no one came to answer. Being a determined little girl, Jewel made a fist and pounded on the door as hard as she could. Soon it opened a crack. "What do you want little girl?" The voice sounded like that of an old man.

"I lost my dog. Can you help me find her?" Jewel asked with her sweetest and most persuasive voice.

"I don't see a dog, do you?" was the odd reply. But before Jewel could answer, supposing that the question had been posed to her, another voice said, "No, didn't see a dog this way. Now turn around so I can see our visitor more plainly."

The door opened a little wider and small wrinkled fingers stretched out toward Jewel. "Let me see your hand," the person in the house suggested.

Now Jewel was taught to be careful around strangers, but she really needed to find her dog. The hand was open, held at the height of her waist, and waiting still. Slowly and carefully, Jewel reached toward it, ready to pull back if the stranger attempted to grab her. But his touch was soft on her palm. His finger drew across it, and then tapped upon the tips of hers.

Suddenly the door opened fully. "You are welcome. Please come in."

It was a middle-aged man. He looked somewhat like her father, but was much shorter. They stood there, the stranger and Jewel, almost the same height, each peering deeply into the eyes of the other.

The little man quickly spun around and Jewel saw a similar face on his back. It was smiling at her. She shrieked and the high-pitched sound made their ears pop.

"Please don't be afraid," the other face said. Jewel noticed that a hole had been cut in the back of the man's shirt to allow the other face to show through. The shirt fit tightly around it. It had eyes, a nose and mouth, but no ears or hair of its own.

Jewel took a step backward and intended to run away.

"We have always been this way," the other face said. "You only stare at us because you have never seen us before. Have you ever reflected on your image, how your other self may appear to us, as we see you through your looking glass?" he asked, and then observed, "Of course, reputation is often ill informed."

The two-faced little man spun around again. "Hi. This is Me. What Metoo means is that we are normal here," and he paused, "in fact, you look strange to us, despite what you may think."

Jewel noticed that behind the man was yet another mirror. She saw the other face, Metoo, watching her from his reflection there.

"Do you feel well?" the little man asked. "Only the ill come this way. We're here to tell you to go back home. Don't try to live your life in two places –it cannot be done rightly. You must choose – with integrity, honesty, and true commitment. Otherwise, you will become a two-faced person."

"But I must find my dog!" Jewel began to feel upset as tears welled in her eyes.

"Really?" the other face asked, "What's its name?"

Jewel paused and answered slowly, "Ransome is *her* name."

"Really? Well, I guess she did!" the man chuckled. "But if Ransome ran away, how will you find her? By now Raven has probably captured her."

And he spun around again.

"Don't go on this journey," the second face warned, "or your other self, this self, may not return. We have seen others like you and many do not return to your world," Metoo warned.

This confusing talk was causing Jewel to become angry. She grasped the sides of her skirt and thought about what to do next.

"Vincent… Honey, it's time to eat," a voice said from a parallel reality. His mind spun, not wanting to leave the cottage of Me and Metoo. "Vincent, it's important that you eat something."

"But I'm lost!" Jewel moaned. "I don't know the way home."

"Then you must consult with the three-eyed frog," Metoo advised.

And the man spun around again.

29

"He's a toad and a wizard," Me corrected his other self.

"No, he is definitely a frog," Metoo argued from the mirror.

"A toad!"

"No! A frog!"

"Well, what's the difference and who cares anyway?" the old man frowned as he stiffened his shoulders. This action seemed to wrinkle Meetoo's nose.

Jewel found their bantering to be humorous and her mood quickly changed as she laughed softly to herself.

"You will find him at the shoreline of the Great Lake... Go right, left, right, and..." the voice faded away.

He moaned as light brightened and the groaning of the mechanical lung filled his ears once again. He tried to move but his body did not respond. A hand touched his forehead. "Vincent, everything's okay. Just try to relax. You were having a dream, but you're back with me now," the nurse smiled reassuringly. "I'll give you a minute, and then you need to take your medications again. Is that okay?"

Vincent pondered on his strange dream. What was the journey and why would he not be able to return? What if the two-faced man was telling the truth? He wondered if his mind was just playing tricks or if he should heed this warning. Surely, he wanted more than anything, to return to his prior life.

CHAPTER THREE

The authorities didn't know how Polio spread. It was estimated that ninety-five percent of the local folks contracted the disease and that the vast majority of them were carriers, contaminating others. But only a few would be stricken as badly as Vincent was.

Granny Em came to visit every day for two weeks, holding onto the hope that the nurses would change their minds, and believing that she would be the first to hear the good news of her grandson's recovery. But there was no such announcement. Still, she clung tightly onto faith, and hope. The nurses would tell Vincent that she was there, peering through the window at the end of the long corridor. He couldn't see her, but he felt her presence and prayers. One day she brought jars of strawberry jam and gave one to each of the nurses, hoping and praying for them to relent of their rule and allow her a quick visit. It would be the slightest of indiscretions, to overlook a brief reunion.

When they finally convinced Granny that the isolation ward would not be breached by a visitor, she began writing letters. Every night before she went to bed, she wrote Vincent a short note that was delivered the next day. Granny told him about their relatives and friends, even noting the weather, which he had no awareness of as he could not see outside. She described beautiful sunsets, refreshing showers, the arrival of blossoms and bees, and the mother robin that persistently fed her new hatchlings. And there were updates on the coming June crop of strawberries: which fields looked the most promising, when rain was needed, how Pops was getting along with the help, and more.

Granny was instructed to write on just one side of the paper so that her letter could be posted above her grandson's head. It would remain on his reading board until the next one arrived.

Her writing kept him connected, as a force that mends broken links in the chain of life, the life he needed to desire still. Vincent realized that hope cannot be lost, or all is soon gone, but he was struggling to hang on.

In that hospital ward, his mind drifted away as his spirit desired to flee. He was weakened by the endurance required to survive each and every day as the disease lingered. Dreams brought the relief he needed.

#

Jewel turned to go, with a hop and a skip, and then stopped to wave goodbye to the little man and his other self. She felt that they had become friends and wondered about their warning of Raven. She should have asked more about this creature. It sounded to be threatening.

Although this two-faced man was strange in his own way, he - they - seemed to be honest, not saying things to be manipulative for gaining the listener's approval, but sincerely different; yet their disagreement was funny.

As she walked a shadow crossed on the ground in front of her. It had the shape of a large bird, wings outstretched. She quickly ducked beneath a lilac bush and watched the giant fowl float away on the wind. It should have deterred her, but Jewel was a strong and determined little girl. She swallowed her fear, gathered her wits, and determined to march on. She had to find the three-eyed frog, the wise wizard of this strange land. Her footsteps quickened and then she began to run, paying close attention to the splits in the trail, and remembering the directions given by Me.

Soon the weeds along the edge of the path became higher and the ground became soft like a sponge; it squished water out from under her shoes. Towering over Jewel were giant catty nine tails, their brown plumes like that on a soldier's hat when wearing his dress uniform, the mass of them as a squadron suitable for a king, or a wizard. The sun sparkled on the water visible through the reeds.

She arrived at the shoreline of the Great Lake.

Jewel shaded her eyes with her hand held against her forehead and squinted at the sun's reflection as it shimmered on the water. She saw lily pads and large yellow flowers with thick pointed pedals floating on the lake. There was a slight breeze and ripples formed on the flat surface, rolling away like an army marching in straight rows toward enemy soldiers hidden on the opposing shore.

Leaves rustled and she heard a buzzing sound. A large dragonfly flew by. Its wings were clear film, its eyes dark red balls that seemed ready to pop out of its head, and its body an iridescent blue color, shining in the bright light. The dragon fly darted back and forth and headed toward the lily pads.

And then it was gone.

His tongue snapped like a whip and snagged that fly, recoiling to deliver it into the frog's large mouth, an appetizer before dinner. The motion of it caused the frog to twist and turn slightly on his raft that consisted of a large lily leaf. Jewel distinctly saw his three eyes, lined up in a row, straight across his slimy forehead.

"Hey you, Mister Three-Eyed Frog," Jewel called and waved her hand at him. The critter looked her way and gently paddled in the water with his webbed feet to adjust his view, but he made no response to her calling.

"Well, are you a wizard, or not?" Jewel challenged.

These words aroused the frog and it leaped into the clear water. Jewel watched him swim into the deep, his legs forming a fan that he pushed outward to propel himself forward like a torpedo. She strained her eyes to follow him, but he soon disappeared in deeper, murky water. She waited

33

and watched. She waited some more, and began to be afraid that the frog had fled to his castle for safe refuge. Surely, she reasoned, a wizard must have such a place.

Suddenly water splashed into her eyes and the amphibian popped out of the lake, landing on a flat stone, directly in front of her. A chorus of cicadas buzzed in announcement of his appearing.

He stood tall and wore a purple cape that hung loosely around his long, hugely muscular legs. On his head was a hat, a tall cone, also purple in color with a yellow crescent moon surrounded by stars that glittered in the sun. His left hand held a staff, topped with a large diamond. This he grasped tightly with his long fingers and as he tapped it on the stone a laser beam shot upward into the azure sky, exploding there like fireworks.

All three eyes were clearly focused on the shocked little girl, as Jewel gasped in amazement, stunned by his beauty and performance. She instinctively bent her knees and curtseyed before his royal highness.

"Be at ease little girl," the wizard instructed. "Your respect is noted, and accepted," he continued. The center eye lid closed momentarily as he considered his next question. "How may I be of service? Have you lost your way?" the frog asked with intuition.

"My d, do, dog," Jewel stammered, feeling insecure.

"Was he a puppy still, black and white in color?" the frog suggested. "Raven has caught him, I saw him carried overhead, clutched by the beast's talons. The poor little dog was whimpering like a baby."

"Oh no!" Jewel shouted and began to cry. "It can't be! Tell me it isn't so."

"What is your dog's name?"

She sniffled and said, "Her name is Ransome."

The wizard frowned. "That explains it. Raven has kidnapped your puppy and is holding her for payment. He is a foul fowl, and tries to intimidate us. But his power and influence are limited."

34

"What should I do?" Jewel demanded as she shifted on her feet. "What can I do?"

"Oh my, dear, oh dear!" the wizard stroked his white beard that suddenly appeared. "That vulture is incomprehensibly inconsiderate and insensitive to your concerns. Dear, oh dear. I don't believe you will be able to pay his ransom."

"Please!" Jewel pleaded. "You are wise. Please think even harder. There must be some way that I can get my puppy back."

"Well, there may be one way," the wizard remembered and stroked his beard again, as it suddenly grew longer, reaching all the way to the ground.

"It's a magical berry. If you can find it and eat it, your nightmare will end. You will immediately be transported back to your prior life, to your home, with Ransome too. But getting that strawberry: not an easy task. It is an arduous journey that will lead you to the berry patch, and there is many a peril."

Jewel nodded and the wizard continued. "The wild strawberry grows at the bottom of Angels' Landing, a butte composed of pure citrine quartz that encompasses many precious stones. The berry patch is alongside the pool at the foot of the waterfall. These cascading currents tumble down from five thousand feet above, the top of the butte. When the moon is full and bright, a moonbow forms at the foot of the waterfall, lighting upon the patch of berries. You must pick the one that was touched by the spectrum of beautiful color dispersed by the moonbow."

Jewel's mouth hung wide open and she spoke not a word, gasping in wonder at the wizard's description of a place that must be too wonderful to be true.

"It's really the most beautiful place you will ever see," the wizard warned. "But don't be enthralled by it, consumed by its charms, enticed by its luring, or you will never return home," he emphasized the point with a single finger held high in the air, and then concluded his statement, "I

35

visited there once, and barely escaped with my life." The balled tip of his long, slender finger slowly returned to its place alongside the others.

Jewel returned a puzzled gaze.

"We each have our place in this world, and our time to serve, just as I am here now, for you. We must fulfill our destiny. That requires courage and determination, but we will only know redemption upon completing the intended purpose of our life. So, you must not be bamboozled, to be deterred from it!" Realizing that he was nearly shouting now, the three-eyed frog lowered the volume of his voice and continued to teach the little girl.

"The dishonesty of deception is a subtle influencer," the wizard warned. "If you do not make a choice, a firm commitment, you will become two-faced," and he paused for effect but then continued to make his main point, "We cannot serve two masters, for we will be devoted to one and despise the other," and he concluded with an asking, "I don't want to be the one despised, do you?"

Looking deep into Jewel's eyes, the frog saw confusion with his most perceptive, center eye, and knew that she did not fully understand his question.

"Do you know how fast you are moving right now, even as you're standing still?" the wizard was getting chatty and decided to test her with some trivia.

"Well," he continued, "We're on a carousel that is spinning at a speed of one thousand miles per hour, and it's not stopping to let us off. I say giddy-up to every morning, a new beginning, to do and say the right things."

There was a pause, as the wizard waited for her to respond.

"Why is it called Angel's Landing?" Jewel finally found her voice strong enough to speak again.

"No one has ever been to the top of the butte," the wizard said as he told the tale shared by millions of critters for thousands of years. "It is said to be the place where Heaven touches the earth. The angels are messengers, guardians, and warriors. They come to deliver blessings for the people of the world."

The wizard's beard was now so long that it curled upon the stone and began stacking itself into a coil that grew taller.

There was a rhythmic sound like that of a beating drum, or was it a giant clock? Her time with the three-eyed frog wizard was coming to an abrupt end.

It was the banging of the nurse's thick heeled shoes, painted with whitener to promote cleanliness, which echoed in an adjoining hallway. Miss Jenkins, Supervising RN, was about to begin her shift. A clock in the hospital's foyer with Westminster Chimes sounded the three-quarter hour for six in the morning.

"But how do I get there?" Jewel asked anxiously. "Which way is it from here?"

"You must cross the Great Lake," the wizard instructed as his beard began to recede. "Go to the beach on the south shore."

Jenkins yanked on the heavy door that was the entrance to the isolation ward. She pulled on a cord that slipped from her hand and a window blind shot upward, slapping the glass as it spun around the spring-loaded dowel that anchored it there. Daylight spilled into the room, an unwelcomed interruption for those sleeping in the metal cylinders. The nurse reached for a wall switch and fluorescent tubes

37

made the room instantly bright, their soft humming unnoticed, masked over by the whooshing noise of the air pumps.

A black cloud moved away from the sun and the lake's water again reflected a stunningly bright light. Jewel's pupils constricted and the appearance of the wizard dimmed before her. The sound of the wind rustling through the reeds suddenly became much louder. The frog turned to face the lake, squatted and leaped into the air, his costume disappearing before he hit the water. And with a BIG splash, he was gone.

Nurse Jenkins strolled down the aisle between the rows of polio patients, their bodies aimed in opposite directions so that their heads were at the center of the room, along each side of her walkway. Like the crankshaft driven movements of a machine, her head turned swiftly, side to side in a timed fashion, checking for signs of life among the souls caged there. She stopped at Vincent and tapped him on the cheek. "Com'on Sweetie, back to reality."

He moaned and turned his head away. With his eyes still closed, he sought a replay of the dream, desiring the mystical land of the moonbow, a place serviced by angels. Vincent wondered why he could not, why he should not go there, for surely it was better than where he was, better than his sad existence in that awful place, his hell on earth.

The nurses would soon begin their rounds with medications. This day he needed an extra dose.

CHAPTER FOUR

For others in Vincent's family, life continued with the persistence that was required for survival, despite the tragedy that had befallen them. His grandfather, Frank, had the mammoth task of toiling in the fields, but this work was about much more than income; it promoted true prosperity, perhaps in more ways than he knew. A true sense of satisfaction came from his purpose in providing for others.

His loyal customers anxiously inquired for the start of berry season and were waiting for his arrival at the farmer's market, anxious to greet him on his first day. By the time he parked the truck and set up his table, a line had already formed. He sold out every Tuesday and Thursday night at the town square.

"Hello Mrs. Johnson," Frank greeted his first customer.

"Well, I'm glad that you're finally here," she said in response. "Seems like a long wait since last year."

Frank nodded. "The weather was cooler this spring. Less sun. But the crop is good."

"Two quarts please, and a jar of jam, if you have it."

"Certainly," the farmer confirmed as he pointed to a pasteboard box that sat on the tailgate of the truck, directing his assistant there. "And how is John doing?" he inquired politely.

"He's got it bad now, you know, having a hard time breathing. Spitting up black mucus when he coughs," she frowned hard as her chin dropped and her face became as stoic as a stone sculpture. "A miner's plight. Black lung…" she whined, "just doesn't seem fair."

40

"Well, I hope some fresh produce will cheer him up," Frank offered a smile as he handed her a basket full of strawberries.

Mrs. Johnson shifted on her feet as she waited for her change. Frank smiled again and thanked her sincerely as she nodded and moved away.

Next, his eyes met those of Jerry Kravitz. He was a family friend, a retired welder first introduced by a cousin. Jerry had been the life of their parties. He played the fiddle, always had an Irish jig that floated off his horsehair bow to arouse a joyful mood, and then would challenge his friends with a hearty joke.

Frank offered his hand in greeting and grasped Jerry's firmly. "It's always good to see you, my friend."

Jerry's eyes brightened, but lacked the luster of days gone by. "How you doin' Frank?" he inquired, intending to direct attention away from himself.

"Good, we're doin' good."

"And Emma?" he quickly added.

"My wife's still cooking up a storm," Frank admitted and patted his large belly with a gratifying smile. He paused and looked into his friend's eyes, seeing discouragement there. "But how is Betty feeling?"

She was a high stepper those days of joyful gathering, leading the way for a square dance as she pulled others into the circle. It was an appropriate response to her husband's making of merriment.

Jerry looked down and squinted as a teardrop fell to the ground. He tried to contain his emotions, but just as enthusiasm had been freely exhibited upon their greeting, sadness was evident now.

"Oh, you know," he swallowed hard. "Betty has some good days," Jerry attempted a smile. He paused, "mostly bad ones though," and looked away, blinking hard again. "Today was a better day," he cleared his throat. "She sent me here to get some berries. Making a shortcake. I'm happy to see her on her feet in the kitchen," and his face cracked with a grin.

"Is she still getting chemo therapy?" Frank asked slyly.

"No," he answered firmly. "No, her treatment is ended."

"Give her our love," Frank affirmed, "you know that she is in our prayers."

"True friends," Jerry agreed as he made eye contact and nodded. He gathered his purchase and prepared to leave.

Frank sold seventy-five quarts of strawberries that evening and was feeling tired after his fifteen-hour work day. He sighed as he started the truck. The plight of his friends dominated his mind. Emma was home making cakes and jams and anxiously waited for Frank's return, and the news he would bring.

Frank dropped to the caned chair that sat in the corner of the kitchen as it squeaked under his weight. He began untying his work boots. They would be deposited there, under the chair, confining the dust and dirt of the field to that single spot, a routine he had repeated for thirty-three years.

Emma watched impatiently, a dish towel in her hand. "Well?" she inquired, hoping for good news.

"I saw Mrs. Johnson," Frank began his report. "She wasn't too optimistic," he reasoned, "guess old John is hanging in there though."

Emma nodded with understanding. "Well, who else did you see?" she asked again.

42

"Jerry," he said, "I saw Jerry. I don't think Betty is any better though," he admitted reluctantly, "probably worse."

"Well, what did he say?" Emma continued her interrogation.

"Not much. He seemed emotional. Delicate."

"Oh, that's too bad," Emma conceded.

"But Betty is in the kitchen and doing some cooking," Frank recalled. "Perhaps," he paused, "there is still hope."

"Of course there is! As long as we are breathing God's good air, there is always hope!" Emma almost scolded him as she began putting utensils away, neatly placed in their designated spot in the drawer. "His Spirit gives us life," her words drifted toward the open window.

Frank nodded and got up to walk down the hallway to the living room where his easy chair was waiting.

"Did you make my deliveries?" his wife interrupted Frank's retreat.

"Sure did," he answered quickly, "The box with shortcake and berries to the Robinsons and jam to the Sicklers."

Emma turned to face him, waiting for details.

"Robinsons' son, I think Jeffery is his name, answered the door, and Sicklers' house looked dark so I left the box on their porch near their front door." His words faded as he stepped into the hallway. It seemed that his curious wife always had a need for conversation when he lacked the desire to say anything more. She could shoot questions at him like the rapid firing of an automatic weapon. Frank was looking for his book, a history on the Civil War.

Emma grimaced as she returned to her sink. "Guess I'll have to call them," she instructed herself, intending her husband to hear her sentiment of disapproval. She looked out the kitchen window to the faded sunset, orange strands lingering there among the grayish layers of clouds. "Lord have mercy," she prayed softly as she dried her hands on a dish towel. "Give me the strength to keep going," she paused in reflection, "and help me be a blessing to others," she requested in quiet reverence. "So much pain…" she sighed while in deep reflection.

It would be little more than an hour until Frank would begin the arduous trek up the steep stairway that led to his bedroom. Their home was a modest Cape Cod style house, the upper rooms crammed into the attic space under the steep roof enlarged by dormers. Frank and his father, Joshua Abel Vandenberg, built the house with hand tools: saws, hammers, chisels and shovels. It was a two-year feat.

The basement, only five feet in depth, was dug by hand. Water trickled across the dirt floor most months, infrequently disappearing in August if it was a dry summer. Shelving covered the end wall and was filled with pint and quart size glass mason jars with Ball lids tightly sealed and containing canned produce from their garden, their winter's food supply. In the center of the small, dungeon like room, a single bulb hung precariously by an electrical wire that offered a short pull chain to its operator. Once illuminated it would swing back and forth, casting eerie shadows on the stacked stone walls and alerting any critters that may have taken refuge there to immediately retreat. A musty smell dominated the unwelcoming place.

Frank's proper name was Merritt Franklin Vandenberg, but he preferred the shortened form of his middle name. Few people knew his full name.

On nights after attending the farmers' market, Frank's routine was to unwind with a chapter from a book. He was a history buff, and preferred

44

detailed reports of the ravaging skirmishes of the Civil War. His great-grandfather had fought in the Battle of Antietam and lost his lower left leg there. Although Frank had never met his acclaimed relative who died shortly after the war ended, he heard many tales about him.

This night he was likely to nod off before completing even a few pages. Emma would finish the dishes in the kitchen and then gently nudge the arm of the man she devoted her life to and firmly believed in, toiling day in and day out, along his side.

#

Another house hidden under large oaks stood a short mile and a half away from Frank and Emma's quaint abode, but the difference between the two was like the contrasting light of day and the darkness of night, good intentions and evil desires.

The paint on the window sill was cracked and blistered, showing obvious signs of years of neglect, evident even in the light of a half moon, dimmed by the clouds that chased each other across the night sky. Next to it, a bearded man sat at a desk, a decrepit piece of old furniture, gouged and broken, with one half-leg resting upon a stack of two cinder blocks. It was illuminated by the room's ceiling fixture that had a fan above a single forty-watt bulb attached there without a glass globe. The blades of the fan wobbled as the motor grinded and they rotated near the ceiling, casting shadows for a flickering on the man's tabletop. Dust particles floated to the boards of the wooden floor below where they would conglomerate in wide cracks.

He carefully held a round object in his left hand, between his thumb and forefinger. He looked through a magnifying glass held in the other hand; its first finger was shortened to the second knuckle by an unfortunate accident.

His hands were rough, blistered, nails chipped and cracked, with dirt stains in the crevices. His facial features were exaggerated: a large nose and huge ears. His eyebrows were like an untrimmed hedge row, its wild sprigs hanging low, these thick gray hairs nearly pricking at his glossy eyes. His beard was as an abandoned field, filled with weeds and thistles spurs; not edged, but burly, and matted from saliva drooled there as it encroached upon his lower neck. Blotchy skin bagged under his eyes and wrinkles rippled toward his cheek bones, the top of them connecting with the ridges of his forehead. They resembled a series of waves racing to the shoreline when there is a brisk wind.

A bottle of whiskey sat near the edge of his desk, one quarter of its contents still unconsumed, its lid lying on the floor near the baseboard after falling there and rolling toward the wall.

Old Joe Mansfield raised pigs in the thickets behind this decrepit house. With five breeding sows from last year's brood surviving winter and a sassy boar, it looked to be a promising harvest for him this year.

When ignoring the hogs, he gathered fallen limbs from dead trees for firewood and scoured the area around his place for scrap metal, hoping to find an old appliance dumped on the bank along the roadway. His lane came to a dead-end about two miles further down the hill, near the creek. This was a popular fishing spot and offered secluded parking for couples who were all heated up, mostly high school seniors. It was rumored that a crazy person stalked the place late at night. Some people wondered if the tall tale could be true and if the peeping tom was Joe.

46

Lovers once died there, in the boy's car, discovered late in the afternoon of the next day. It had been a chilly night and the car's engine was still running when they were found. Their demise was attributed to carbon monoxide poisoning. If a stalker had been nearby, he did nothing to save them.

Joe was Barton's father, his old man, but certainly not by choice. It was the fate of his birth right, their position in life, and both resented it. The two of them scratched out a meager existence at the homestead, the front room of the shack the remnant of a surviving log cabin, said to be one of the original settlements in Sweetened Vales. But the area was not called as such back in the day of its first settlers. It was known as the Northwest of Clayton County. Of course, all that changed later on.

Bart was said to be the great-grandson of a bank robber, whose face once adorned a most wanted FBI poster, wild-west style. This rumor was also popular among those who resided nearby. It was retold and circulated through the community at least twice yearly.

With a whoosh, the sound of rushing air, a large black bird landed on the window sill. His dark eyes shifted quickly, from side to side, as he ducked down low enough to clear the opening and hopped inside the house. This caught Joe's attention. He dropped the gold coin and magnifying glass on his desk as he turned toward the bird. It squawked and jumped into the air. With a single flap of its wings, it lighted on a perch made of tree limbs. It held a metallic object in its beak.

"Ah Raven, my old friend," Joe greeted the fowl, "what do you have for me today?"

The crow shook its head and hopped again.

"You want a peanut, don't you?" He pulled out the top desk drawer and reached for a treat, searching for one not already shelled by the mice that shared this accommodation. Raven grunted as Joe tossed the peanut into the air. The bird dropped the shinny object and stretched its neck long enough to catch its reward. It shifted to a single foot and placed the peanut in his beak. Balanced there, it began to rip apart the nut's outer shell, tossing the remnants of it in all directions.

Joe lunged for the contraband Raven had delivered. As he bent over the bird jumped onto his back. This caused the old man to lurch forward and spring upward, spinning on his heels while swinging his arms in the air; but he could not reach the creature. Raven had a firm grip on his shirt, his claws piercing the cotton material and needling at the man's spine. It seemed that he enjoyed the ride, holding his wings out to glide through it. As Joe threw his back against the wall hoping to crush the fowl it escaped and went back to the window sill.

The man's language was ineffable, profanity rolling off his tongue like a dog's rage at the postman who knocks at the door unannounced, finally coming close, after daily visits to the box out front; the distance always annoyed the beast.

Raven once clawed at Joe's face. He thought the large bird intended to gouge his eyes out.

"This is crap!" he yelled and threw the broken earring, inexpensive costume jewelry, at the crow. "Get the hell outta here and fetch something worthwhile!" The bird squawked in reply and returned to its perch. It was finished hunting for the night. It eyed his adversary and watched for other signs of aggression. Each hated the other and flaunted superiority, willing to engage in a fight when necessary.

Granny's next letter to Vincent in the hospital, said she hoped for a bumper crop and that she would be extra busy once the berries began to ripen on the vine; and she promised not to forget her grandson. She said that Nurse Jill consented to allow him to have a taste of her strawberry shortcake.

One day while Jill was feeding Vincent he decided to ask her some questions. "Will I ever get better?" he queried.

"Vincent, I have some good news for you today," Nurse Jill began. "Your baseball team won again last night," and she offered him a tarnished spoon with a cube of red Jell-O wiggling on it.

But he didn't care much about sports that day. Despite the breeze generated by a fan nearby, he continued to sweat, feeling like the lobster dropped into an iron kettle. But his discomfort was more than the sweltering heat, sticky air that smothered him; it was confinement. He longed to run playfully down a woodland trail, to again explore the great outdoors, to experience the freedom of his dreams.

As his face turned upward, his eyes were tightly closed, his lips pursed. The nurse watched intently. Her patient blinked and a tear appeared. Like an inmate escaping, it ran down his cheek through the open area seeking a place to hide and took refuge as it pooled inside the base of his ear.

"What's the matter, Honey?" the nurse asked sympathetically. "Com'on Vincent. You're a trooper. No, you can't give up now. I won't let you."

He slowly turned toward her and blinked hard, releasing several more imprisoned tears. He sniffed as his nurse reached for a tissue. She dabbed at his eyes and ears.

"But will this ever end?" the boy asked. "How much longer must I suffer like this?"

"Now you know I don't have such answers," she responded with resolute calm. "And you know what the doctor said... right?"

"No. No, I don't," Vincent moaned as his eyes met hers.

"Well, I remember," Nurse Jill reaffirmed confidently. "Most other symptoms of the disease have disappeared," she smiled broadly to emphasize this positive point.

"But when... when will I get out of this thing?" he complained. "Will I ever be able to walk again?"

"You must be patient," the nurse now whispered as if she was revealing a secret. "One day at a time," she reminded.

Vincent turned away and his crying increased momentarily.

"Vincent!" she spoke louder to demand his attention. "There are good signs. I still have hope. We have to have a little faith."

Nurse Jill knew more than she was saying, withholding information so as not to raise her patient's expectations to a dangerous place of vulnerability.

The doctor suspected that his lungs had a thirty percent capacity for breathing, and soon Vincent would begin therapy sessions, outside the lung. Even a normal person could hold his breath for a full minute. The time outside the iron lung would test and press upon his natural ability to increase his breath, but it would be painful. Vincent would have to be a strong solider. She would help him overcome his fear. Another pill would numb the pain, and yet another would decrease anxiety.

"Let's give it another week," his nurse said, "seven more days. Perhaps then you will be stronger," she suggested hoping that he would accept this new goal. "You have the best doctors, and are receiving the best of care," Nurse Jill reaffirmed. "And this lung is a marvelous invention. It is designed to help you and is intended to be temporary. We must be grateful for the life we have, and the healing God gives. His grace is sufficient," she preached. "His grace is sufficient for each day."

Her patient responded with a long sigh, his spirit reviving slightly.

"Now you must be a strong little solider," she urged. "You are doing the hard fight. Keep going… for your mom," she suggested, and then remembered, "and for Granny."

At the mention of his loved ones, he smiled slightly and Jill padded his forehead with a damp cloth.

"Hey," she urged in a happy tone. "Speaking of your Granny, she is bringing in a special treat for you. Maybe tomorrow. You know what it is?"

And his smile broadened. "Yes," he replied softly. He turned his face toward hers, still pleading, "Thanks for your kindness," and Vincent offered the best smile his crushed spirit would allow.

That day she gently kissed his forehead and asked if he had a secret food desire, something other than Granny's shortcake. It was 7 Up, which she brought in a tall, clear glass. He sipped slowly from a long straw and watched the tiny bubbles as they rose to the surface of his sweet liquid joy. But all too soon it was gone, so he closed his eyes, once again seeking refuge in his secret place, an adventure known only to him.

#

Jewel stared in disbelief, hoping the wizard would reappear. After waiting several minutes, she started to walk along the Great Lake's shoreline. Soon, she came upon a vacant rowboat bobbing in the water. With the sun in her eyes, she pushed off and began rowing. It was then that she realized that she was seated in the wrong position as she remembered her uncle who had taught her to sit facing the rear of the skiff, to row backwards. This was a more efficient way of breaking the wind, but now it was too late to move without rocking the boat. Yes, she was afraid of tipping it over, because she was *not* a good swimmer.

#

Granny Em was very anxious to take fresh strawberry shortcake into the hospital for Vincent. It would be hand fed to him while in the mechanical lung.

Other children had already left the ward, but Vincent's paralysis continued and his prognosis was poor.

Pops estimated that the first row of berries would be ripe for picking in three days.

It was Wednesday evening and since Frank didn't have to go to market, he decided at his wife's urging, to visit Hank. In a paper sack she had carefully placed two quarts of berries and a Bisquick shortcake.

Near the farm at Sweetened Vales was an old Victorian house, its origin dating back to a time before the Civil War. The old man lived there with his only daughter, Julianne.

As a little boy Vincent was shy but would smile upon seeing her, playing in her yard with her puppy. She would stop and wave to him. He would quickly turn away as his heart leaped for joy, but he was too embarrassed to acknowledge her.

Frank traversed the short walk up the dirt lane to the home of Hank and Julianne Culp. He continued to the rear porch. The door there was wide open. He rapped on the screen door that slapped at its jambs. He could hear the shuffle of a person inside.

"Oh, it's you," Hank said without a proper greeting. "Well, you might as well come on in." He held the screen open. "Okay?"

Frank stepped into the rear of the kitchen. Recently modernized, the cabinets connected to a countertop that formed a short "L." This peninsula was topped with red and green checkered linoleum and edged in shiny metal, secured by nails. It was supported by a post at its end and jutted into the open space there. On the other side of it was a sitting area with a large picture window that afforded a view of the roadway.

The cabinets, recouped from the old pantry, were whitewashed in many layers of paint. They received a fresh coating annually, but a few chips revealed the many years of their existence, and an earlier layer that was a cream color.

"I had a nice gold piece, a gift from my father," Hank noted as he led the way to the front parlor. "I was looking at it on my desk, there, next to the window. But now, I can't find it," he lamented, "I must have misplaced it. It was a liberty head gold eagle, a ten-dollar coin."

Frank shrugged in reply and looked around the room before returning his attention to his host. "You look like you've lost some weight," he suggested.

"My gut ain't any good. I can't eat anything that doesn't bother me," Hank explained. "Doc says its ulcerative colitis. No cure. No real treatment. Have to nurse it along. That with my bad back, keeps me pretty much in the house, almost immobile," Hank whined.

"I'm so sorry," Frank said with sincerity. He looked at the paper sack he still held. "Perhaps you don't want Emma's cake then?"

"Oh no, I'll munch on it, and Julianne will want some." Hank grabbed the bag and sat it on the counter top before motioning toward the front room. "Let's have a seat. Take a load off." He dropped into an overstuffed chair, a cloud of dust bursting into the thick air. "I ever tell you the story about my descendant who fought in the Civil War? He was with the raiding parties that went into the Deep South, after Lee surrendered."

Frank shook his head and quickly looked for another chair. He had heard rumors from others who claimed to have heard Hank's tall tale. Some said he was hiding the treasure, but Frank thought Hank likely just talked too much.

"When Jefferson Davis fled for his life the Confederate treasury had $500,000 in gold coins," Hank stated enthusiastically. "Worth half a mil back then. Just imagine what that gold would be worth now! And, that was just the beginning of it!"

Frank returned a questioning look.

"It's true," Hank defended, "I did my research. I looked it up. Assets of banks in Richmond, Virginia, the Confederate capital, gave the Rebels another $450,000 in coins. The Treasury Train left Richmond in a hurry on April 2. That was 1865. They were headed to Georgia, with plans for the President, Jefferson Davis and his cabinet, to eventually board a ship in Florida and escape with the loot."

Frank appeared to be impressed with the details of the historic event. Most of it he could verify with knowledge gleaned from his reading.

"Lincoln was already assassinated by then," Hank elaborated. "Everyone was in a turmoil. The coins alone would be worth over $15 million dollars today. They planned to take their government out of the U.S., reestablish themselves, and keep the country divided – even expand their empire."

"Yeah," Frank admitted. "I heard that they hoped to move into Mexico, maybe even Central America."

"That's it!" Hank agreed. "But the Yankees had already invaded much of the south and as the money was transported by train and wagons, headed for Georgia, various units of the Union Army were closing in from numerous points. Union spies had also infiltrated the ranks of the men charged with guarding the Confederate treasury."

As Hank paused, Frank shifted in his seat.

"My great-grandfather was a Union soldier sent into Georgia at that time," Hank continued. "I never knew exactly what he did there because he wouldn't tell. But he always claimed that there was lots of money, gold and silver coins, gold bunion, and a treasure chest of jewelry that was quickly divided up, and then, some of it taken by bandits. Union spies and defected Rebels conducted raids. Some was confiscated by the Union Army, and then lost again, unaccounted for. Most of the coins were never found."

Nodding in agreement, Frank grinned. "I've heard that."

"You know the Colonel who built the mansion up on Black Rock Mountain? I've always wondered where his sudden wealth came from – and how much of the stash, especially the gold coins, were taken north, maybe even through this territory. I mean heck, there could be some of it buried right here."

"It's fun to imagine." Frank scratched at his arm and sighed as he looked to his feet. "But tell me, where did that coin you said you misplaced come from?" he inquired hoping to come back to their present reality. "And do you have more of them?"

"Nope, and don't know," Hank answered quickly. "It was passed down from generation to generation, to my father's father, then to him and to me. You know, it's dated from before the war. Could have originated from anywhere, I guess."

The duo, long time neighbors and friends, caught up on local gossip before there was a lull in their conversation and Frank reached for his hat in departure. "Sure hope you're feeling better," he said in conclusion. Hank appeared tired and offered only a slight nod in reply. Frank nodded too, and looked toward the kitchen. "I'll show myself out," he said and waited a moment longer. Hank had apparently lost himself in his thoughts. "Goodbye my friend," Frank offered before walking away.

CHAPTER FIVE

A stem and leaf protrude upward, stretching toward the sun. A small white flower with soft pedals suddenly blooms and awaits pollination.

A crack forms in the clouds that darken the sky. A beam of sunlight traverses the expanse of the universe and settles upon this singular strawberry blossom.

There is a gentle breeze as the miracle of life continues with a sprinkle of light rain. Caught by the sunray, a rainbow forms.

From within the arc a droplet reflecting light refracted and displaying the full spectrum of majestic color is dispersed, falling gently upon the little flower with the insemination of blessings.

The metamorphosis the strawberry blossom undergoes is a miracle of the Creator's intent to provide luscious fruit containing a sweet essence, and the power to heal.

#

Several days later many berries were bright red in color. Pops quickly filled a quart basket, pinching off the stem of a large one and placing it on top, headed for Em's kitchen.

It was like a factory of confectionery delights, highly efficient and productive. She moved quickly in a robotic fashion, not distracted by anyone or anything. Within an hour her small round table in the eat-in kitchen was covered with cakes in metal pans, still steaming hot. Some were made with the help of Betty Crocker using Bisquick, while others were a scratch made cake, course in texture. And then, there was Vincent's favorite, the soft, sweet, sponge-like cake called Angel Food. Pops preferred the real homemade cake, she liked the Bisquick, but today she had Vincent on her mind. With each mixture of egg whites, flour, sugar, and vanilla, she offered a silent prayer for his healing.

While they were in the oven, Emma would wash, sort and slice the berries. Next, they were mashed in a large bowl and sugar was added. The experienced cook did not use recipes, but knew the ingredients and their amounts instinctively, the entire process refined by years of production.

She tasted the juice and added some more sweetener. This factory used large amounts of sugar and butter.

The juicy berries were placed in smaller serving bowls and quickly refrigerated. They were kept separate, to be applied at the time of serving Emma's delicious dessert.

She glanced at the clock. It was already 2:30 PM. She quickened her pace. Visiting hours at the hospital ended at four. This was the day for delivery.

Jewel paddled the boat quickly and began to perspire as a breeze cooled her face and rippled the waters ahead. Clouds appeared suddenly and joined together, blocking the sun's rays. She opened her eyes wide in search of her destination. How far could it be? The south shore was barely visible, merely a wide, white line, way off on the horizon.

The wind grew louder and stronger. Then, within a few short minutes, everything changed. Waves suddenly formed, wearing white caps as they lifted the bow of her little boat and then dropped it into a cavern of swirling water. They splashed and her shoes got wet, quickly soaked as the lake began flooding into the flat bottom of her little boat. The sky grew darker still.

Jewel squeezed the handles of the oars and continued to row, even as the wind spun her sideways and waves tilted her upward, lifting her higher and higher.

Crack! Lightning flashed nearby and Jewel screamed as she nearly slid off the wet seat. As she leaned one way, the oar on the other side lifted and its peg popped out of its holder. She dropped it just then, and saw it rushed away by the raging wind and current. "Oh no!" she yelled and paddled as hard and fast as she could with the remaining oar, wanting in hope to straighten the direction of her craft before the water crashed against it once again.

She saw it coming, the largest wave yet. She held tightly onto both sides of the boat, hoping to steady herself, but there was nothing more she could do to prevent what happened next. The little boat was lifted still higher by the giant wave and then flipped over, spilling the little girl into the churning water.

Jewel heard air gurgle and then all was quiet. She waved her arms but continued to sink into the deep, her hair stretching upward as it reached for the surface.

Water splashed on Vincent's face as a nurse began her morning chore of bathing the patients in the lung ward.

Jewel tried to scream for help, but words weren't possible under water.

Vincent's eyes popped open. Still frightened by the dream, he gasped for air.

"Hey there little man, try to calm down," the nurse said, "everything's okay." She watched terror fade from his eyes as he returned to his dismal but safe place. And then he remembered the promise of the day, Granny's treat. But would it be as good as he hoped for it to be? Could it be even better?

Vincent would later recall the experience as follows, "I've got to tell you, my grandmother really outdid herself that day. The shortcake was brought to me at suppertime. Nurse Jill spooned it into my mouth in small bites, telling me to eat slowly and it was absolutely delicious: the berries fresh; the cake soft, its bottom soaked as it absorbed the sweet juice and then layered with more berries; all topped off with her homemade whipped cream, smooth and luscious. Just thinking about it makes my mouth water. I wish I could enjoy it again, right now! I savored every bite, as it made me feel more connected to my past life, which I knew before I was struck with polio."

Perhaps it was at that moment that he turned the corner in his battle against the disease. Energy surged within him and his spirit was renewed. With a revived determination, Vincent possessed a new desire and hope for recovery.

That night the dream continued.

\#

As she sank even lower a strange peace came over Jewel. Fear was gone. Remembering her Sunday School lesson, Jewel said a prayer for rescue, and in her mind, she saw Ransome, curled up in her wicker bed, sleeping soundly without a care in the world. She watched a school of yellow fish swim by, apparently not a bit concerned for her well-being. And then large bubbles began to appear and attach to her body.

Rokoes are invisible until they expel H_2, becoming purely O. As one came near to her face Jewel saw it more clearly. It had the usual round shape, its outline obvious, but upon a closer look she could see its other features: four short legs, a crooked mouth with two large front teeth, the lines of a tiny nose, and large eyes, smaller circles spaced far apart.

The bubbles multiplied quickly. There were ten, then probably a hundred, and then maybe a thousand. They lifted her and as Jewel began to rise toward the surface, she heard a very soft, faint sound like a chirping noise, but much quieter than that of a songbird. She lifted her head and saw the light above becoming brighter.

With a splash and a cold chill, Jewel broke through the surface and realized that she was floating, flat on her back, upon a breeze. It was taking her, still surrounded by bubble like Rokoes, toward the south shore.

The sky circled above, clouds raced by, and a sunbeam lighted upon her face. The horizon changed colors, going from dark gray to bright blue. A crescent moon appeared there, still faint in the light of day.

61

Jewel was astonished at her good fortune, an immediate answer to her prayer, a saving that even she could not fully comprehend. This was such a strange place.

She closed her eyes and felt the warmth of the sun drying her forehead and hair, now streaming alongside her face. She heard air rushing by and then a popping noise.

At first there were only a few pops, and then many more, in chorus, an anthem to the disappearing Rokoes. Her feet slid down and gently touched the warm sand of the shoreline.

And Vincent suddenly wiggled his toes.

Jewel darted across the sandy beach, now barefoot, quickly jumping away from a sharp stone. A shadow came over her as a large black bird swooped down from above, its talons fully extended. She ducked in the nick of time to avoid being grabbed as the feet of the flying beast combed through her hair and scratched her scalp, the top of her head. Jewel stumbled toward some more stones and then regained her balance while looking into the sky. There she saw Raven, his evil eye focused on her as he circled back, intending to dive at her again.

Ahead was a forest crowded in front by a thick patch of huge Musk Thistles. They had wide leaves with jagged edges covered in long needle-like thorns. Contradicting their threatening appearance, each was crowned with a large and beautiful purple flower. Jewel ran with all her might toward the big, ugly weeds.

Raven's shadow came once again as a warning. Jewel dropped to the ground and the bird skimmed above her back, tearing her dress. Too low to recover flight, he crashed into the thistles, screaming in agony. Black feathers and fluff shredded by the thorns burst into the air as Jewel spun to her left, tripped, and fell. The last thing she saw was a parting of the thistle

62

stems and a naked bird hopping out, its skin plucked. Raven leaped into the air and flapped his mangled wings but dropped back to the ground. He screeched as he called to his cohorts, allies in his domain of evil.

It was just then that Jewel fell backwards into a pit, spinning in a circle, watching the opening above become smaller and smaller as she dropped deep into the earth. Then her head jerked back as she landed into fury arms. Something had caught her and cushioned her landing. In a dim light she focused to see who or what it was that held her.

Just then Vincent woke suddenly and sensed that something was different. His feet felt warm. He called for a nurse.

"Vincent, quiet down!" she commanded as she ran toward him. "It's late and you'll wake up the others." She began checking his vital signs. His pulse at the jugular vein was rapid but not fast enough to be of concern. His temperature at his forehead felt normal to her touch.

It was 2 AM and other than the sound of the pumping of the mechanical lungs, all was quiet. She was whispering now. "I'm going to get you some medication. Please, you must keep quiet. No more hollering."

As he wondered about the strange feeling, something he had not felt since stricken, the nurse returned with a pill and a glass of water.

"Here, take this," she instructed. "It will help you sleep. Okay?" She reached toward his mouth and he opened it instinctively. "There now, I'll stay here until you drift off again. It was probably just a bad dream."

All she could see was a large round, black thing. She touched it and felt something like a wet sponge. It twitched. Jewel reached farther and saw

63

eyes aglow as they glistened inside with a beam of yellow light. Two small round ears emerged from the back of its head.

Jewel squinted and rubbed her eyes. Her feet touched the bottom of the pit as the creature gently stood her there.

It was a marmot, a giant whistle pig!

It was taller than the little girl and much rounder. It looked to her intently, but spoke not a word. It dropped to its four large feet that had very long claws and stepped away. Twitching its tail at her face, it looked back and seemed to smile.

Jewel took a hold of its tail, intending to push it away, and just then the whistle pig stepped forward, pulling on her arm. She grabbed the tail with both hands and squeezed. Suddenly she was pulled off her feet, then airborne, as the whistle pig ran through an underground tunnel.

Whisked away like a rocket blast, the earth surrounding her in the passageway became a blur as she was quickly pulled through it. The whistle pig flicked its tail again, jerking her just in time to avoid a collision with a protruding stone. Roots, as fine as hair, tickled as they rubbed against her arms and legs.

"Whoa," she yelled. "I can't hold on much longer." But the whistle pig ignored her plea and continued to race through the twisted channel.

"Really!" Jewel warned as the tip of its tail curled around her wrists and squeezed. In its grip she relaxed some.

Light increased and Jewel noticed more roots and stones. Then she was propelled into the air, an open space below the glowing of a full moon. She fell into a patch of moss and stood just in time to see the whistle pig wink at her before it dove back into its burrow.

Apparently, she had arrived, but where?

It took a moment for Jewel to come to her senses. The air was cool. She heard the sound of rushing water.

The butte reflected the moon, shinning like silver but reddish-brown in color. The waterfall glowed, whiter than new fallen snow, its intensity fading against the mountainside as it sprayed upon its surface. The sky was radiant alongside the ominous facade, its color a deeper blue than anything she had ever seen before. She bent her head back, wanting to see the top of the butte, hoping perhaps to see an angel in flight, but only a star beamed back from the Milky Way, hung there like an ornament on the top of a Christmas tree. It was anchored somewhere millions of miles away, in the vast universe beyond.

Jewel gasped at the beauty of it all. But it was the intense colors, the refracted light of the moonbow that caused her spine to tingle as she shivered in awe, covered in goose bumps. A mist rose from the pool of crystal-clear water at the base of the mountain and shined in the light: amethyst, inspired by the colors at the bottom of the moonbow. The polychromatic arch shimmered in the gentle breeze as it touched upon a patch of wild strawberries.

Overwhelmed with joy, Jewel fell to her knees and silently watched as the glory of it all settled upon her like a warm blanket. She felt content and fulfilled, wanting nothing more than to remain there, in the presence of elegant glory.

CHAPTER SIX

October arrived that year with wonderful color: bright yellow poplars, dark red maples, and the nearly fluorescent orange of the pumpkins when the sun shone directly on them from its lower position in the horizon. The early pumpkin harvest came just in time for Frank to make a final trip to the market. It was closing day for the open-air produce store and a glorious day it was: seventy-five degrees, full sun, with happy tones everywhere. And to his customers' joy, Emma had found a pasteboard box and filled it with twenty ½ pint size jars of homemade strawberry jam – great for a breakfast topping on pancakes or French toast, better on buttered homemade bread that is still warm right out of the oven, and best on vanilla bean ice cream. It was a confectionery delight that never went out of season.

Another peddler swooped in as soon as she saw Frank place the box on his truck's tailgate. She purchased the first jar of jam and then flaunted her prize by carrying it throughout the square. A line quickly formed at the rear of the flatbed from Sweetened Vales, and Frank became busy, although the pumpkins, as pretty as they were, garnered much less attention.

A large calloused hand extended toward him. A welcoming gesture, it was a greeting, a friendly handshake from an old friend.

"John!" Frank exclaimed with great enthusiasm, "John Johnson, well it sure is good to see you!"

"Good to be here, old buddy," he replied with a broad smile while pumping Frank's arm to emphasize his enthusiasm for the greeting.

"I saw your wife in June," Frank remembered. "She said you had it bad then."

"Much better now," John answered. "Thanks for asking. The cough still comes during the night sometimes, but most of the time I get a good, uninterrupted sleep," he informed. "Need the rest."

"Great news!" Frank exclaimed. "Em will be so happy to hear it."

"Not just me," John informed. "Seems the folks around here are all gettin' better, almost like there's a miraculous healing, or something."

"Well thank Goodness for that!" Frank cheered.

"It must be all those delicious strawberry desserts we're eating," he said jokingly as he patted his stomach. "Gained a few pounds too."

"I always say," Frank responded with a smile, "love is the main ingredient in Em's cakes and jams," he paused and scratched at his forehead. "She says it is His blessing."

#

The blue planet tilts on its axis during its orbit around the fiery star. Seasons change and winter claims its place with a cold chill.

It seems that time has slowed despite earth's wild race, moving 67,000 miles per hour to complete its annual orbital path, a loop consisting of 584 million miles.

Another year concludes with 31 million moments of mankind's striving, forever gone, relegated to their past, now part of their memory banks.

#

Next spring in early April, there was a celebration held in the fellowship hall, a covered dish dinner. The crowd of elderly folks was much larger than usual or expected. Many in attendance had not been there during the previous year's event.

After they sang several old hymns accompanied by the piano, Jerry Kravitz broke out his fiddle and played Morrison's Jig. There was a stunned silence, and then feet began tapping as everyone clapped, but the high stepping of this song was much too vigorous for this crowd. Jerry was simply showing off, again.

The last note of the violin's melody faded as the pianist began to play a traditional waltz, "Moon River," a song that speaks of a couple's commitment, "chasing after our rainbow's end."

Jerry carefully placed his instrument on the top of the piano and offered his hand to Betty who without hesitation stood and accepted his invitation. It was a public display of the deep affection each felt for the other. They embraced and gracefully glided across the open floor as they slowly shifted and slid their feet in unison with the tempo of the music. It was a display of the harmony they shared as each humbly submitted to the other, life's mate, with unfaltering devotion. They felt the years, nearly forty if counted, layered upon them with kindness, as they travelled through time together. Tears glistened in the corner of Betty's eyes. She was grateful and invigorated, feeling life at its very best.

And just then there was a whispered notion, much like the sharing of a rumor, and it floated on the lips of others in the room as it spread throughout. "Isn't it true that the doctor gave Betty only three months to live? And that was nine months ago? Well, it's a miracle!"

As the proclamation was spread from person to person, the revelation of its meaning became known and the words reverberated louder and louder each time they were repeated. Old Bertha nodded as Linda enunciated the message close to her hearing aid. "It's a miracle that Betty is still alive."

And just then Bertha shouted at the top of her lungs. "We are being healed… it's a miracle!"

Emma slowly stood and a hush fell across the room. Without words she demanded and immediately received the respect as given to a king's herald. "I have a thought," she offered and reached into her dress pocket to retrieve a small piece of paper.

"Do not judge a song," she paused and added, "or a person, for that matter… by its duration nor by the number of its notes. Judge it by the way it touches and lifts the soul." She paused and looked at the faces around the room. Her dear friend, Ethel, was nodding in agreement.

"When something… or someone… has enriched your life," she continued and returned a quick glance toward her comrades, "And when its melody lingers in your heart, it remains unfinished, because it is endless. Such joy endures for all eternity."

Emma bowed her head as if praying and everyone waited with baited breath in silence as she still stood in their midst. "We must give thanks to God for the mercies He hath bestowed upon us. I love this verse of prose," she stiffened and cleared her throat before reciting from memory, "As the dawn mists over the horizon and the sun closes its evening shade, He is always near."

Emma smiled broadly while saying, "Thank you," and reached for her seat before carefully lowering herself. As she fell softly onto the pad of the folding chair, silence endured until Jerry picked up his violin and began playing a few measures of a familiar refrain. After a short introduction, he sang loudly in invitation for the others to join in the song.

"Summer and winter, and springtime and harvest, sun, moon and stars in their courses above, join with all nature in manifold witness, to Thy great faithfulness, mercy and love."

"Great is Thy faithfulness! Great is Thy faithfulness! Morning by morning new mercies I see. All I have needed Thy hand hath provided – great is Thy faithfulness, Lord unto me!"

"Please join me in the last verse," Jerry interrupted the song briefly.

"Pardon for sin and a peace that endureth, Thine own dear presence to cheer and to guide; strength for today and bright hope for tomorrow, blessings all mine, with ten thousand beside!"

CHAPTER SEVEN

Another day dawned and others in the lung ward opened their eyes, woefully greeted by it, but Vincent's remained tightly closed. His complexion had darkened. His brain resisted the surge of oxygen pushed into his chest by the movement of the machine's levers.

70

Busied with her morning routine, the nurse had not noticed his critical condition as he slipped away, into a comatose state.

There was an enticement in his dream to remain in fairyland, where his unconscious fight for survival was at its weakest. Peace presented itself there.

But still he knew, from somewhere deep down inside, that he must fight on, to claim the healing potion or remain ill stricken, perhaps even die; and what then?

The nurse noticed that Vincent was unresponsive and rushed to his side.

And sitting at the table in her kitchen all alone, Granny was praying for his continued healing.

Suddenly the nurse was yelling for help as another summoned the doctor.

Falling into a trance, Jewel dropped to the ground and began sleeping. But morning would not awaken her, as the night persisted in this place. It was always dark here, summoning the weary to a peaceful slumber.

She dreamed about her dog, Ransome. Her puppy was the reason for this journey, to rescue it, and the vision was a reminder of that, and more so, an urging to return home and to complete her mission.

In her dream Jewel saw the dog prancing in front of her with a toy held tightly in its mouth. Jewel reached for it, a wide smile forming on her face, and giggled as Ransome lurched backward. The puppy challenged her to a game of 'catch me if you can.'

Jewel reached for the toy again, faster this time, but the dog ran away. Within seconds Ransome returned, darting back into the room, passing quickly by, her ears floating on the air as she cut through it, her paws airborne more than then they touched the floor, a devilish look in her little eyes. Ransome jumped over and dodged the obstacles in her path and Jewel laughed in amazement of her skillful maneuvers. She expected the dog to crash into a chair at any moment as it continued to circle and whiz by. But then Ransome suddenly stopped, sat directly in front of the little girl and dropped the prize of the game there, on the floor, as she panted heartily.

Jewel laughed.

She longed to see and play with Ransome once again.

A light breeze cooled her face and Jewel revived some. It was a Guardian, blowing gently upon her.

"Jewel," it whispered. "Wake up my little angel girl. Your time of lasting repose is not yet come, for now you must return home."

Jewel opened her eyes and caught a glimpse of the creature that floated there, before it disappeared, vanishing like the mist before the sun. It was formed by triangles joined together, with a head like a box, an upside-down triangle that pointed upon the face separating its eyes and spreading them wide apart. Its head was surrounded by thick dark hair that formed a point on top. Its dress was soft velvet with sequins that glittered in the moonlight, and it held a wand in one hand.

She gasped and as her breath misted upon the cool air, the Guardian faded away.

The doctor was holding an oxygen mask against his face, covering his nose and mouth, when Vincent's eyes suddenly popped open. They were filled with fear. He coughed and jerked his head away to free himself of the mask's confinement.

"He's coming around," the doctor announced with relief.

Jewel gazed once again at the waterfall, the moonbow, and the strawberry patch. With purpose renewed, she was gripped by determination. She slowly rose to her feet and looked intently, focusing on the ruby red berry illuminated by the bow. She began to walk that way and took her eyes off of the prize only long enough to find her way around the boulders. She scrambled over them. Lifting her head from the pathway, she again focused on the berry. This time, nothing would deter her from her mission.

She pinched its stem and held it high to reflect the moon's ray. It was beautiful, shimmering and shining as if bursting with life. She placed it upon her lips and the sweet aroma of healing filled her nostrils with tantalizing desire. In her mouth it was soft and cool to her tongue's touch. She bit down gently, felt its juices squirt against the sides of her mouth, and her mind began to spin as she was consumed with the berry's luscious flavor.

Jewel closed her eyes and when the dizzy feeling subsided, she opened them to find herself sitting on her living room floor. Ransome was sitting there too, anxiously staring at her as if the dog was concerned.

"We're back," she whispered. "Oh Ransome, I'm so glad to see you."

The dog panted and a drip of saliva fell from the tip of her tongue as it drooled from her mouth. Her eyes brightened like the flickering of a candle in a dark room. There was happiness there. Her excitement was obvious.

Jewel grabbed her puppy and hugged it tightly. "Welcome back." She released her hold and looked into the dog's longing eyes. "I really love you!"

#

To the surprise of his doctors, Vincent was completely cured by the age of twelve, but was it a grandmother's love, or a greater blessing that healed him?

Three years later, at the age of fifteen, he began working with his grandparents on their farm, picking stones, planting, hoeing, and picking and packing berries.

CHAPTER EIGHT

Vincent's formative years, as a young adult...

"Honest work establishes the man." These were the words Pops used to admonish his grandson the day Vincent began working on the farm. "In honest work we don't just make a buck, we establish ourselves and build a good reputation," he continued, "Be a person that is free from debt."

Frank looked at his grandson, a strapping young man, and felt pride swell within. He paused, wiped the sweat off his brow, and continued, "When you earn it, it is truly yours... yours to use as you please. No one can take it from you. You will always enjoy the fruits of your labor."

That afternoon, the boy, now yearning to become a man, rode on a metal seat that lacked any padding for comfort. The contraption pulled by the old John Deere M was manned by two. The beveled edges of the metal plow formed a narrow furrow. When the machine clicked, a rider quickly placed a young strawberry plant in the ground. Water squirted in and the narrow trench was closed by angled blades in the rear. As Vincent reached to the crate for another seedling, it was his partner's turn to do the planting. And so they continued, row after long row, to sow the entire field which encompassed five acres.

He'll never forget that day when he reported for work and she was there, standing near Pops in the field. She was sixteen then, more mature, enticing. They were eager teenagers.

She came to the field because her father, Hank, desperately needed extra money. He was ailing at home. Although his ulcers were slowly improving, he was unable to work and the family's savings were nearly depleted.

Vincent would walk with her as she returned home at the end of their work day. She shared the stories she heard from her father. A distinguished Civil War colonel who retired nearby to a mountain resort with a mansion was said to be a confidant of her great-great-grandfather. In another tall tale her ancestor was a spy for the Union, penetrating Confederate territories and eavesdropping on officers of the Rebel government. And there was the rumor of Civil War gold.

One June day she asked Vincent if he believed in angels. Enthralled by her presence, consumed by her glory, he could only say yes. She reached for his hand and held it gently. They came upon a large mossy boulder poised under a giant oak. "Let's take a break," she suggested, "We can rest here, but just for a minute. I've got to get home to make my Daddy his dinner."

Vincent nodded with understanding.

They sat there not speaking a word, but gazing into the sky, and then imagined animal figures in the great blue beyond. She pointed out a kitten, a unicorn, and then she found her angel.

"Vincent?" she inquired softly and squeezed his hand. As he turned toward her, their eyes locked in a gaze that peered deep, even unto their pleating hearts. She leaned toward him and closed her eyes. Still wondering, he felt her lips touch his, and then also closed his eyes, letting his mind swirl unto a mystical place previously unknown.

Vincent felt the kiss release and opened his eyes to see hers twinkling with delight. It was her first kiss, innocent and pure, sweet sixteen!

They looked back to the sky expecting to see Cupid there. A large bird was soaring on the wind, tilted and flew overhead, momentarily casting a shadow upon them.

Vincent had once encountered the crow while delivering Granny's goods. It was at the Mansfield home, where Barton and his father Joe lived. Their reception, to say the least, was contrary to what was appropriate and expected in response to an act of generosity from a friendly neighbor. A rifle was fired into the air and someone yelled in warning. Vincent could not be sure which one of them it was, but suspected the old man. Frank instructed his grandson to stay away from their property. Emma objected to the exclusion but submitted to the directive of her husband's unrelenting demand for their grandson's safety.

One day, not long afterwards, Barton walked to the farm and requested work from Frank. Other than the rumors, little was known about his folks who kept to themselves. The less than anxious applicant refused to answer questions. It was only Pops who was willing to give him a chance, and so Barton came to work reluctantly, with a hard heart.

"Why would you hire him?" Vincent asked one afternoon after Barton disappeared from their sight. He had already left for home.

"The boy has his problems, no doubt," Frank reasoned as he stroked his chin, deep in thought. "But many of them were not of his own doing," he declared.

Vincent returned a confused look.

"He doesn't have to own what his father does," Pops continued. "He needs to find a way to escape from his heritage. He's still young. Let's give him a chance. Maybe he will decide to be a better person."

But Vincent didn't appear to be convinced, looking at the ground, slowly shaking his head. "I don't think we can trust him," he objected. "There must be someone else you can hire," he paused as he felt he might have overstepped his place as the younger, "isn't there?"

Pops returned a stern look and a long sigh.

"I really don't trust him," Vincent reiterated. "He acts one way when you're watching, but what do you suppose he is saying and doing when our backs are turned?"

Pops pushed his hat back and scratched at his hair line, deep in thought. "I wouldn't say that he is two-faced, at least not yet. A person becomes two-faced when they begin lying to keep a secret. Perhaps one of the hardest things in life is learning to live truthfully, knowing when to disclose more of what is held in confidence, but never pretending to be someone or something that we aren't."

"But, but…" Vincent objected, but then began to perceive the greater meaning, the truth of his grandfather's spoken words. It silenced him.

"We all have our crosses to bear," Frank elaborated. "In speakin' the truth, we find sympathy and understanding, but in lying for a secret we will only know deception until it increases and consumes us."

"How do you mean it?"

"The lie changes our focus. Our lives are no longer an open book, but have the cover of deceit. Maintaining our other self, the self that is established in such deception, becomes our purpose. Don't let a secret tangle you in a web of lies," the elder, wiser man admonished. "We lose some of our humanity, even our capacity to love, when we continually hide behind secrets."

The next day, Thursday, was again market day. For Vincent it was a special occasion when he was chosen to accompany Pops into the city where they were greeted with enthusiasm and heard stories from his customers. If someone was feeling better, Pops always gave credit to God, even if the person was a non-believer. He would remind them of the nourishment of his berries, a gift of the Creator. It was his privilege to be the taskmaster of the fields and the provider of simple blessings.

Even after all the produce on their folding table was sold, others who heard a recommendation would come and request the fruit of his fields, the labor of his hands. But Frank had sold out. Spotting a carrier with quart baskets full of berries still on the truck bed, eight in all, someone pointed and demanded that he sell them. Next to it, there was also a pasteboard box containing several small jars of jam. "What about them?" the man demanded. "I'll buy them."

"They're not for selling," Frank explained. "They're for giving, and I'm sorry, but they're already spoken for."

Vincent's grandparents knew of others who continued to suffer and prayed diligently for their blessing to be received. It was a time when people really cared for each other. Granny Em possessed little but generously shared what she did have: strawberry jam and fresh strawberry pie when it was in season.

#

It was a hot June day in the beginning of the month, the third year he worked at the strawberry farm. Vincent walked toward the packing shed with a carrier of berries, eight full quarts. He saw Barton talking to Julianne. Although Vincent could not hear their words, she was frowning and showed fear, as her body language indicated "no!" She turned her head from side to side, looking for help. Barton reached for her hand. As she withdrew, he grabbed her wrist. She tugged against his grip, obviously wanting to get away.

A few strawberries fell to the ground as Vincent quickened his pace, almost running. "Hey Bart," he yelled. The couple continued to argue and pull at each other. "Bart, leave her alone!" Just before reaching them, she broke loose and ran toward Em. Barton snarled as Vincent came closer, then shoved him backwards, causing him to fall. The carrier dropped into a row of plants; the baskets nearly emptied as the berries scattered on the ground. He looked like a monster standing above Vincent, silhouetted by the sun that was positioned behind his back. His shadow, appearing as that of a giant, reached far into the field.

"You little weasel," he snarled. "Can't you see it? She likes me. She's my girl," Barton growled.

"No!" Vincent managed as he raised himself with his arms braced behind his back and looked for his feet. "She doesn't want you!" he wailed. "I saw her trying to get away from you!"

Barton leaned over his rival and pointed at his face. "She's mine. Stay away!" and he paused, "or else," he threatened.

Twenty cents per quart – it was the wage of the strawberry picker, a tedious, back-breaking job. The picker entered the field at 8 AM, got a thirty-minute lunch break promptly at 12 noon, and continued to work until at least 4 PM. The best pickers could fill more than 100 quart size baskets each work day. They were constantly on their feet, bending at the waist, and pinching off berries with both hands, reaching for the carrier to gently place them in the baskets only when both cupped hands were full. The berries were held gently, so as not to bruise them. The picker, a young man or woman, nudged the carrier forward as it sat on the straw covered aisle, about eighteen inches wide, between the rows of strawberry plants. They often worked in the full sun all day long. They carried no snacks or drinking water into the field. They were allowed to refresh themselves from the community water bucket when a full carrier was taken to the packing shed. A couple tin cups were attached to the half-barrel with twine. The need for hydration served as additional motivation to fill their baskets quickly.

Em received the carriers and on a sheet of paper kept a tally for each picker. She quickly surveyed the baskets and offered advice such as, "pinch off the stem and leave only one-quarter of an inch," or, "the berries have to be fully ripe: fully red without any blemishes, but not rotten or partially eaten by a slug."

Three dollars – it was the hourly rate for the packers and the straw boss. After updating the picker's record, Emma pushed the carrier on the narrow counter top toward a packer. The packer's job was to quickly rearrange the top of each basket so that it was most appealing to the buyer. They used another container of berries from which they selected large ones to replace any that were not up to their standard. They were constantly tossing the rejects behind them. The luscious berries quickly formed a mound that extended two inches above the basket's rim.

Frank busied himself with inspecting the final product, supervising the packers, loading the flatbed truck, supplying additional baskets and carriers for the pickers, and consulting with the straw boss. Of course, he had to tend to any other immediate demand the farming business interrupted him with.

The straw boss was an older teenager, often able to drive if he was needed to run an unexpected errand, but his job was primarily to supervise the pickers in the field. He carried a long stick and used it to push back the leaves so that he could determine if the picker was collecting all the ripe berries. He was vigilant against anyone being idle, eating berries off the vine, or throwing them at someone else. It was the first and oldest trick to place stones in the bottom of the basket and the boss was always watching. He moved constantly, sometimes hopping over the rows, to sneak up on a picker he suspected of an offense. Filling baskets with stones, excessive eating, and loitering, was reported to Frank and that picker was usually dismissed immediately upon approaching the packing shed with a carrier.

The carrier was handmade by Frank in his workshop during the off season. He disassembled old crates for the material needed. The ends of the carrier were shaped from thicker wood and formed a rectangle at the base with a triangle on top. Near the very top was a hole that contained the dowel, the handle that connected the two ends. Vertical strips of narrow wood were attached to the front and rear edges of the ends, spanning a distance that was just the right length for four quart baskets to be comfortably placed in a row. There were two rows in the carrier, separated by another narrow strip of wood that went down the center. And then Frank added its bottom, long slats of crate wood trimmed and nicely fitted on the bottom of the rectangular ends and spanning the length of the carrier. Everything was attached with small flat head nails, carefully pounded in by a hammer so as not to split any of the wood. Frank soon learned that it was necessary to drill a pilot hole down from the top of the ends into the handle so that the nail could be placed to secure it there.

Repairing the carriers and replacing them with newly constructed ones was tedious work as the farm required an inventory of about one hundred. Frank approached this chore late in the fall after the plants were mowed over and covered with straw, the irrigation system was dismantled and stored for the winter, and the most urgent equipment repairs were completed. He welcomed the time spent in his workshop, a large room designated at the end of a larger storage shed, another pole building referred to as the barn. The shop was warmed on days that were unseasonably cold by a small wood stove located near the entrance door. The only electricity in the shop was for lighting, several incandescent bulbs that precariously hung on a wire from the roof rafters where they were stapled. The implements, including the saw and drill, were rusty old hand tools.

After 4 PM the straw boss would holler, "That's it for today." The pickers urgently topped off any partially filled baskets and went to the packing shed to complete their day's tally. A line quickly formed there. Those most determined to prove themselves, likely competing with a peer, lingered in the field to fill all the baskets in their carrier. The most aggressive pickers paced themselves so that they took eight empty baskets into the field at 3:30 PM. They would be the last in line at the packing shed for the final count.

Finally, they all walked down a lane to the entrance of the farm where there was a small parking lot. They lingered there, joking and teasing each other, until the old Chevy truck was seen bouncing down the alley riddled with stones too large to remove. Frank exited with a small gray cash box and placed it on the tailgate. He paid each picker in cash, with the exact change, according to the notes on Emma's roster. He would call a name and state the total number of quarts picked, as that person stepped forward to receive his or her day's earnings. Some left quickly while others lingered to learn of the achievement of the best pickers. This public announcement promoted a competitive spirit among the farm workers. Occasionally Frank would comment on a picker's achievement, especially if it was a new record or a milestone for that particular person.

CHAPTER NINE

That night only a dim light burned in the rear room of the Mansfield shack. Both Joe and Barton were out on the town.

Sharon Clemow, a widow attractive for her age, was a young 43. She lived alone in an old farmhouse on a large wooded lot. Her dog, a Beagle named "Butch", was barking at the rear door.

"Quiet!" she yelled from the TV room, but the dog growled and continued to bark, intending to warn his master of the intruder. Sharon reluctantly pulled herself up from the recliner and walked to the rear of the kitchen where the dog was carrying on. She pulled back the curtain of the nearby window and peeked outside. Butch got excited and jumped at the door.

There was a full moon glowing brightly in a cloudless sky. "I don't see anything," Sharon complained, but just as she turned toward the dog a shadow shifted. She held the curtains apart even wider as she gazed intently into the night scene. Perhaps it was a tree limb swaying in the breeze. "No one is there," she instructed Butch and with her foot pushed at his rear paws. "Down!" she ordered. "Quiet now."

Old Joe carefully tilted his head to see around the tree with one eye as he hid there in Sharon's backyard. He hoped she would soon be retiring, and if he was lucky this night, she would be taking a bath.

She thought about calling the police station but quickly decided against the idea, remembering how they shamed her the last time she was frightened. There was no local police department and the State Police located some thirty miles away would likely not even respond to her call about a stalker until the next day. They told her that they had to prioritize calls and responded to emergencies first. "Yes, of course," she agreed while feeling humiliated. She should get an alarm system, they said.

Sharon walked into the parlor and turned off the television set. She picked up a magazine and looked at the cover. It was enticing enough to fold and tuck under her upper arm. It would give her some reading while she soaked. She started up the stairs.

To the stalker outside, the bathroom window was suddenly brightened by the ceiling light in the small room. The window shade was still up.

Joe smiled broadly, his rotten teeth exposed, his smell and appearance enough to repel any nearby critters that were already fleeing into the woods.

Hank had fallen asleep in his easy chair while listening to the radio in the living room. Julianne lay in her bed reading a novel. Her bedroom window was raised. The movement of cooler air was refreshing after working in the fields that day under the hot sun. Her blouse was still sticky from the sweat.

Suddenly she was startled by the sound of rushing air as a large black bird, a crow, landed on her window sill. It grunted as it looked directly at her. "Swoosh away," she yelled instinctively, but when it remained there she tossed her paperback book in its direction. Raven turned and jumped into the night sky.

Julianne rose and rushed to the window, hoping to see its retreat, but there was no sign of it in the bright night sky.

Barton was crouched behind an old chicken coup and felt the beating of his heart quicken at the sight of her. He did not move a muscle or make the slightest sound as he focused on the young woman he fantasized about almost continuously. His pulse pounded in his ear like the beat of a base drum in a marching band, commanding advancement.

She reached for the bottom of her shirt and pulled it up, over her head.

Bart squirmed, so excited he could hardly contain himself.

That was Tuesday.

The next morning Vincent was waiting for the old flatbed truck to arrive at the field and was already daydreaming with a smile plastered across his face as he admired Julianne from a distance. Barton saw his grinning and increased his pace as he walked directly toward his adversary. He stiffened himself for the blow and rammed Vincent so hard he nearly toppled, jarring him back to reality.

"Hey, watch where you're going," Vincent shouted. But Barton did not make a reply, turned and headed for his girl. Just then the truck arrived and Julianne went for Frank.

She held back as her boss began assigning the pickers to certain rows. His eyes met hers and he saw her anxiety. She was sent to the adjoining field, as far away from the boys as Frank could manage at the time.

It was another scorcher, 90 degrees by mid-day, with humidity that stayed above 80 percent. The afternoon dragged on and the strawberry pickers appeared to be suffering under the sweltering mid-day sun.

Frank quickly conferred with Emma and they decided to quit an hour early. She began to inform the pickers that the empty carrier they reached for would be their final one for the day. Everyone welcomed the news.

"Emma," Julianne pleaded, "I'm feeling a little bit dizzy."

"Okay, take a break. You've done enough for today. Get a drink and rest in the shade."

"Thanks. Sorry I can't keep going." But Julianne was thinking about how to avoid Barton. She felt panic as she worried about waiting for Frank to wrap up the operation and pay the pickers. "Emma," she continued. "Do you think I could get my pay tomorrow?"

The boss's wife frowned but nodded. "Sure honey. You can run along," she offered. "Hope you find a place to cool off," her words faded as she observed the girl's quick retreat. "I'll keep your tally," she said louder.

But Julianne did not respond. She walked briskly toward the path that led away from the field to the parking area. Her mind was racing. She wanted to talk to Vincent. She needed to meet him without Barton knowing about it.

Vincent picked eighty quarts that day, and with sixteen dollars clenched in his fist, he turned to walk home when he saw Julianne standing in the opening that was the entrance to the path that led to her house. She looked panicked and motioned with her hand for him to come to her. Vincent looked back. Barton was still standing in line, waiting to be paid, looking down and kicking at the dry ground. Returning to Julianne, he saw her mouth the words, "come on, hurry," with a hand gesture to emphasize her request.

He quickened his pace but didn't run, hoping not to be noticed by the others. As he approached Julianne, she reached for his hand and tugged on his arm. The two ran together and quickly disappeared from their view. They raced through an "S" turn and then she slowed down.

"Hey what's up?" Vincent asked with a happy face. "Are you okay?" he asked.

She sighed after stumbling on a rock that jutted above the surface. "I think so," she panted. She released his hand and saw a puzzled look come across his face.

"Do you think Bart is a robber?" she blurted.

"No!" Vincent nearly shouted and paused, "At least I don't think so," he said as he quieted himself in thought. "Why would you say so?"

"I don't know," she hesitated and wondered if she should continue to explain her accusation. She looked at Vincent and opened her eyes wide. "My dad has lost something valuable," she explained, "and last night I heard someone outside my bedroom window. I was keeping a watch on the yard and thought I saw him running away from my house."

"You mean Bart?" Vincent asked with astonishment.

"Yeah," she answered thoughtfully. "I think it was Bart."

They were both looking straight ahead, deep in thought.

"I don't like the way he looks at me," she admitted. "I'm uncomfortable being around him."

Vincent nodded. "He has threatened me," he shared reluctantly.

"Maybe I should talk to Frank about it," she suggested and paused. "Yeah, we need to talk to your grandfather about him."

Vincent swallowed hard and continued, "He knows that I don't like Bart," he informed. "But there isn't much more to it than that."

After an awkward moment of silence Julianne noted, "I don't want Frank to think I'm paranoid or something," and she looked to Vincent. "I have to be tough," she suggested, "you know."

He nodded in agreement.

After a few more paces she reached for his hand and pulled him to a stop. "Look in there," she instructed. "See that big spruce tree beyond the hedge row? There's a private spot under it. The branches hang low and the ground's covered with moss," she paused, "soft as a bed."

Vincent was squinting as he looked to where she pointed. He truly wanted to know about her secret place.

"It's there," she affirmed. "Just beyond a little drainage ditch."

"Okay," he drew out the word expectantly, hoping for further instruction.

"I will meet you there Saturday night, midnight," her eyes danced with excitement. "Can you come?"

"Well," he paused, his mind looking for clarity as he became excited. "Sure," he said with the confidence of a commanding officer. "I can come."

"I will give you a signal," she instructed. "Check my bedroom window. If the curtains are hanging outside, then all is clear."

She stepped away quickly and looking back saw a young man stunned but smiling. She took several steps and stopped abruptly. "And will you talk to your grandfather about Bart for me?" She was expecting him to comply quickly in consideration of the offer she just made.

Vincent nodded affirmatively as he saw his girl skip and run away.

It was Thursday that he sought out his grandfather, anxious to air his concern. Julianne had avoided him all day but many times their eyes met and she flashed a big smile back at him.

"Hey Pops," Vincent began, feeling the pit of his stomach. He expected his grandfather to defend Barton, but was greatly motivated to speak for his girlfriend.

Frank had picked up the cash box and was headed for the truck. He paused and leaned against the rear of the cab. "What can I do for you, young feller," he teased. Then his voice became stern, "What do you need Vincent?"

"Can we talk? I mean, do you have a minute."

"Sure. For you, I always have the time." Frank took off his wide brimmed straw hat, wiped the sweat off his brow and scratched at the back of his head.

"It's Bart. He has really been bugging me," Vincent began.

"How's that?"

"Pushing me around. Threatening me. Telling me to stay away from Julianne."

"You're too young to be involved with her," Frank instructed sternly. "Keep it cool for a couple more years," he paused as he looked deep into his grandson's eyes. "Can't you manage yourself around Barton? You got to stand up for yourself."

"Yeah, I know, I'm not afraid of him."

"Well then… What's the problem?"

Vincent paused and looked at his feet. He was losing the argument meant to plead his cause and decided to deal the punch line. "Do you think he is a robber?"

Stunned at the accusation, Frank reeled and raised his voice. "Why would you say that?"

"It's not me. It's Julianne. She told me that Hank is missing things. She saw Bart running away from their house when it was dark outside."

"Well, Hank hasn't said anything about it to me," Frank's voice softened. "I think he would have said something… and that's a serious charge."

"Julianne feels threatened by Bart," Vincent blurted. It was his final attack.

Frank put his hat back on and stroked his chin. "I can talk to her about it," he offered. "If he has the hots for her, well then, she has to let him know that she isn't interested. That should calm him down."

Vincent frowned, his eyes still pleading for help.

"As I told you before," Frank asserted, "we have to give him a chance. A bad reputation is hard, if not impossible to beat. Gossip has the power to mold the life of the victim, especially in a small town like ours. It makes a person bitter, and resentful." He paused. "I won't do that to Bart," Frank continued. "He has been meeting his quota. He's a hard worker." He looked away. "So, maybe he's not my favorite, but before I can act, I have to have something more: firm evidence of wrongdoing."

"Yes sir," Vincent knew that the final verdict had been delivered. He sighed and dropped his shoulders, a sign of defeat.

Frank reached for the truck's door handle, opened it and placed the cash box on the driver's seat. He paused, turned back toward his grandson, and felt the need to reconnect with the boy he loved.

"I do care about you," he offered in reconciliation, "and Julianne," he paused, "and Bart too." He took a moment for reflection. "Keep me informed if anything happens," he instructed and opened his arms.

The two embraced quickly. There they were, a young man reaching for maturity, and his elder, a senior man seasoned by life and hoping to establish compassion with justice, linked in that moment of humble submission to each other.

Vincent thought he saw a tear begin to form in his grandfather's left eye, but Frank squinted and it was instantly gone. He was then troubled at his failure to have Barton fired, and felt a bit ashamed at the same time. He wondered what he would report back to Julianne.

"He won't do it, he won't fire Bart," Vincent told Julianne on Friday. The weekend was upon them and normally he would not see her again until Monday morning, but he was thinking about her invitation to meet on Saturday, and he was hoping with excitement and great anticipation that it would still happen.

"You did it?" she asked, "you really asked Frank to fire him?"

"Yea, I did."

"You did that for me?"

"I tried, Julie, but he said he needs proof."

She smiled, blushed slightly, and looked away. Upon refocusing she noted, "My father believes someone entered our house and took a couple of coins from his collection, those he had on his desk for examination. Another neighbor lost small valuables, believed to have been taken by a house burglar. The thief disturbs little and takes only small, single items."

Vincent appeared troubled as he reflected on the information. "Will your dad tell this to my grandfather?"

"I don't see why not."

"Okay then, I'll tell Pops, I mean Frank," he corrected himself.

"Actually, I think my dad already told him about it," Julianne corrected, with the memory of a visit between Frank and Hank. "It was some time ago that he lost the first coin."

"That's odd," Vincent lamented, wondering if his grandfather had withheld information. Then suddenly, questions that accused his trusted mentor crashed into his brain. He remembered Pop's pledge not to ever mislead him. His grandfather promised that he wouldn't lie for a secret. Vincent clearly remembered his words from a talk they had previously.

"Well, what did your dad say about it?" he resumed his questioning of Julianne.

"Nothing... really."

"Doesn't he care?"

She shrugged and said, "I guess so, well... I really don't know."

And in that moment, Vincent doubted that Julianne was telling the whole truth. The thought aroused suspicion toward the relationship he was forming with her, and it was something he had not previously felt.

The question would persist even after the secret died, its relevance gone, but the breach it caused between two hearts remained unhealed.

"So, do you have anything planned for the weekend?" he decided to change the subject.

"No, not really," she offered no details.

They took a few steps together without speaking to each other. The end of the trail was coming within view and Vincent began to feel panic.

"So… we still on for tomorrow night?"

"You'll have to wait and see," she teased with another shrug trying to appear nonchalant to the suggestion. "Look for the sign," she instructed as they parted.

Monday dawned with bright sunshine streaming through Vincent's bedroom window. It would be another day of hard work, back-breaking labor, but seeing Julianne would bring joy to his heart once again.

Because of an interruption during their meeting on Saturday, two nights before, he felt some lingering anxiety. They had parted too quickly.

He ate a bowl of cereal and watched the clock. He left for the fields ten minutes early.

It was starting time and she had not yet arrived. Frank and Emma came later than usual and seemed to be moving slower than their normal pace. He looked around, seeking their faces in the group that assembled there. But Barton was missing. He scanned beyond, to the trails and down the farm lane. No one was approaching. Julianne was missing too!

"Where's Julianne?" he quickly demanded of Emma in a whisper as he picked up his first carrier for the day.

"Can't talk now," she directed, "We got to get started."

He entered his row reluctantly, with a watchful eye. She still was not to be found anywhere. Frank was going about his routine.

During his lunch break Vincent went to talk to his grandfather, but he was gone. It was unusual, but not entirely improbable. Emma also avoided her anxious grandson.

The day dragged on. At one point in the middle of the afternoon anxiety overwhelmed him. He had to know what was happening. He began to devise a plan. Frank would not be interrupted during the time he paid his workers, so Vincent planned to be the last one in line. He would corner his grandfather then.

"She's sick today. That's all I know," Frank reported.

"And where is Bart, why isn't he here?" Vincent persisted.

"I don't know," Frank answered firmly. "I don't know what happened to Bart."

And the conversation was over before it began. Frank and Emma were packing up and leaving. Vincent suspected they knew more than they were saying. He would press them later that evening for more information, or tomorrow if they weren't available. He felt determined, even commissioned, to find out what happened. He felt jittery inside and a spot in his gut began to hurt.

After dinner he demanded answers, yelled at them, and even resorted to shallow threats. But his grandparents would not give him an adequate explanation.

Despite his efforts to learn more about her disappearance, no one would tell him anything, and the rumors he heard didn't make any sense. Barton and Julianne ran off together? Details were sketchy.

The hot summer days were passing by quickly. The final picking of the season was on July 2, two days before Independence Day. After taking Wednesday off to observe the holiday, Frank busied himself in the vegetable plot, promoting and protecting his chance for a bountiful harvest, and there was the small field adorned in orange, a crop of gourds and pumpkins, his second chance for a cash crop, although it provided a much smaller payday. Autumn would soon be upon them.

Days dragged on and the tension between Vincent and his grandparents continued, felt on both sides. Frank began other chores, performing the duties necessary for preparing the farm for fall and winter. It seemed to Vincent that he was purposely overlooked as a farmhand.

Weeks turned into months. Frank hired a new worker, a middle-aged man who was down on his luck and needed to provide for his wife and kids.

It felt like there was much falsehood in the moral lessons his grandfather had preached. Their shunning reeked of insincerity. What were they hiding? If they were trying to protect him, was it their place to do so, and why couldn't they trust him to decide about Julianne for himself? Had their priorities changed, or had circumstances altered the expression of their generosity?

So eventually, Vincent stopped asking about Julianne.

Perhaps she was regarded as damaged goods, no longer suitable to become a queen in the Vandenberg dynasty. The suspicion of such judgment angered Vincent even more.

Second: REALITY! (Julianne's story)

CHAPTER TEN

Julianne's Road to Recovery

In the months after her daughter's birth, Julianne struggled with the harsh reality of who she was and what she had become. She felt forever changed by what happened at Sweetened Vales and was remorseful at the loss of her hopes and dreams. She had no husband; there was no sweetheart, no wedding bells, no church ceremony, and no honeymoon. She was all alone with her thoughts and disappointment prevailed. Youthful vitality left her and she became like something used, no longer new and promising, but much less desirable. Her life became a daily grind of endless routines.

Her doctor had helped her get past her crisis but now the reality of daily life set in.

She moved to Lancaster County to reside with her Aunt Betsy, a paternal relative and widow of many years. Her father came to visit on weekends and stayed with his girls and sister for several days but without exception boarded the bus to return to his home on Monday morning at 9 AM.

Slowly they forged a new life together.

One hot summer day while relaxing, they sat in rockers in the shade of the front porch watching squirrels scamper near trees in the front yard. Brianna was now fourteen months old and crouched at the bottom of the steps where she found a dry spot of ground. She scribbled in the dirt with a small twig.

"Does he ever ask about me?" Julie inquired still feeling uncertainty with her past.

Hank returned a startled look. "Who?" he demanded and paused for reflection, "You mean that boy from the farm?"

"Yes," she affirmed. "Vincent. Don't you still see him or his grandparents anymore?"

"Oh no, not really," Hank answered untruthfully, wanting to avoid the subject. "They have others working there now. I see the hired help, but don't even know their names."

"Well?" she persisted, "You haven't answered my question."

"He went off to college," Hank noted as he cleared his throat. "Honey, please don't concern yourself with the past," he suggested and patted her hand with his.

"I know, I know," she agreed as she pulled her hand away. "But sometimes I still wonder why he never contacted me," her voice faded with the acknowledgement.

"Sweetie, don't be concerned with them," her father nearly scolded. "I won't let them or anyone else hurt you again."

"But how?" she blurted, "What do you mean?"

"I think they blamed you for what happened," he said slyly, "and they are dreadfully wrong!" he exclaimed. "You didn't encourage Bart and you weren't flirtatious with him," he said while inferring much more than the words he spoke. "It wasn't your fault that it happened. It's not that you were easy… he forced you…"

100

Julie stiffened as tears welled in her eyes. She stood quickly. "Me? They say it was me?" she hollered as she stammered on the words. "Really?!"

"I'm sorry Julie," he whined while attempting sincerity. "Like I said, let's just forget about them." He paused. "You need to get on with your life now."

She trembled as anger consumed her. "I'm going into the kitchen," Julie shouted. "Aunt Betsy needs help with supper." She took a step toward the front door, paused, and turned back toward him, "Dad, you can watch Brianna for me." She caught a sob as she attempted to hide the onslaught of tears. Before he made a response she stormed off. Hank heard her stomping on the steps that led to her upstairs bedroom.

He swallowed hard and wiped sweat from his brow. He felt the indignity of his lie but rallied at the justification. He had spoken for what needed to be done. He had little pride left and clung to the hope of a better future for his daughter, one far from the haunts of Sweetened Vales where he had plotted with Frank and Emma to withhold information from their grandson. At the time it seemed like the right thing to do, because, after all, he had questions about the boy's involvement with Julianne.

As Vincent persisted in contacting Julianne's father for answers, Hank was required to layer lies upon lies and now he felt vulnerable for the web of deceit he weaved. He had to protect himself. He couldn't lose his daughter now, not again.

Julie took a part-time job waitressing at a nearby diner. She knew that the locals were gossiping about her and hoped they would soon divert their attention to someone else, perhaps indulge in a juicier rumor. But they continued to pester her, especially the young men, some making obvious advances. She shunned them, always feeling the shame of the accusation from her past.

The hardest question Julianne endured was the one about her little girl's father. She had rehearsed several responses and preferred the one about him joining the army to become an American hero, and making the ultimate sacrifice for his country. That usually stopped their questioning. If she was in a bad mood, she might simply say, "Well one thing I know for sure is that he's not coming back," and then she'd drop a dish on the table top as she rushed away.

Once Brianna began to crawl and play independently, Betsy offered them a small apartment above the garage. They needed the privacy of their own space, she said, but Julie assumed her aunt was referring to herself. The rent would be reasonable, only $150 dollars per month, and the electricity was included, as the small building at the rear of the property was connected by a wire to the house.

It was a stretch for her financially, but she knew that she had to move on. Julie was grateful for the babysitter Betsy was as she never refused or complained about the little girl's presence.

Brianna was a darling little girl, with curly blonde hair and large blue eyes; she was a ringer for Shirley Temple, "The Little Princess" of television. Brianna seldom cried but was pleasant and always flashed a big smile at a stranger. She began to engage in conversation suitable for an adult, as she spent all her time with them. Julianne and Betsy enjoyed dressing her with little dresses adorned in lace. Brianna had more hair accessories than both of the women combined.

That winter Julianne was asked to be a bridesmaid in her cousin's wedding. She was not close to Stacey, the bride-to-be, and Julianne felt the offer was ordered by her aunt who was always asking about her. Her grandmother's sister, on the maternal side, Aunt Florence, frequently inquired with, "how is she doing? Is she getting along okay? How is her recovery going?" Her interest and concern was overbearing for Julianne. Betsy did her best to shield her from all of it, suspecting that the old woman was determined to get some of the juicy details about what had happened.

Julianne politely said no, noting that she was tied down with her job and taking care of Brianna. None the less, an invitation to the gala event arrived many weeks later. It noted that her little girl was also welcome to attend. Julianne didn't want to go, but lacked a good excuse. She had enough notice to request the afternoon off from work.

A little socialization would do her good, Betsy said.

Julianne decided to skip the church wedding, noting that Brianna would not sit still during the ceremony. Very reluctantly, she went to the social hall where the reception and dinner were to be held. On her way there she wondered who she would sit with and dreaded the requirement of "catching up" with old acquaintances and relatives. Everyone would have their brags, boasting about their achievements and those of their children. She knew of no one else, who like herself, was fighting for their life as she barely existed.

While entering the building she was spotted by Florence who nearly flew to her to begin the small talk required before she could launch into her interrogation. After a loose hug and "Oh yes, we're doing great," and "here is my little angel, have you met Brianna?" she announced that she had to take the little one to the restroom and quickly broke away.

Pulling on the child's hand, Julianne paused at a round table covered in white lace that contained the seating cards. She found hers and looked for table number nine. She was relieved to find it in the back of the reception room, at the edge of the side where the groom's guests were seated. She was pleased to be sitting with strangers.

During the dinner she ate little but occupied herself by constantly doting on her daughter. Half way through, she held Brianna on her lap, using her as a shield against further intrusions or invitations to leave her seat, but Brianna was tugging to get away. The little one had spotted another girl, one that appeared to be the same age, hopping and skipping to the rhythm of the band on the dance floor.

Julianne scanned the crowd to identify her parents. She seemed to be unattended. Brianna squealed and kicked causing her mother to lose her grip. The two toddlers met, drew close to each other, and appeared to making introductions. Julianne scanned the tables nearby. A young man, likely the little girl's father, was glancing repeatedly toward them. Then he began scanning the crowd, doing the same thing Julianne had just done, searching for her. She felt a little embarrassed and quickly looked away, not wanting to be identified.

The band played Michael Jackson's song, "I'll Be There," and the girls held hands and swayed together, sometimes spinning in circles, and giggling all the while. The stranger, the man who was obviously

Brianna's dance partner's father, continued to look around the room. Observing the intensity of his search, Julianne began to smile, her first one of the day. She watched the girls some more. Brianna dropped to the floor, dizzy from spinning. Instinctively, Julianne stood quickly, but Brianna was already back on her feet and chasing after her new friend. When she looked back at the man, their eyes met. She had been discovered.

Julianne turned away quickly. When she returned her gaze, he was saying something to her, pleading with his eyes. She shrugged her shoulders and smiled. He smiled and pointed to Brianna, then to her. "Oh yes," Julianne said aloud even though her voice would not be heard on the other side of the room. Then she nodded, "Yeah, she's mine." He nodded in return and pointed to his daughter and then back to himself. Julianne smiled and nodded again. The communication was crude but they had understood each other.

Julianne decided to focus on the girls instead of the handsome young man who watched her from across the ballroom. But every time she glanced his way he was fixated on her.

A familiar tune began and he quickly stood up. It was the Hokey Pokey and this father was determined to help his little girl with the moves. Brianna also attempted to join in the fun. Right foot, left foot: the girls didn't know the difference. When it came time for their bottoms to be put in they looked stunned and bumped each other before tumbling onto the floor. Julianne chuckled as the man scrambled to put them upright again, tripping, and nearly falling himself.

Everyone was laughing as the music began to speed up. He left the girls and approached her with a hand outstretched. "Come and join us."

Julianne could hear his invitation as he came with pleading on his face. She held up one hand, the stop sign, and shook her head from side to side. He paused, frowned, raised his eyebrows as he shrugged his shoulders and returned to the girls.

The three of them held hands, him bending low to reach the little ones, and danced in a circle, "Ring Around The Rosie" style. And every time he came within view, he flashed his best smile at the beautiful young woman who still refused to join in the fun. But they were having a blast!

He was tall with thick, neatly styled hair that held its place as he bounced around. He clothes looked expensive. His accessories, tie, belt, and shoes were well coordinated. As Julianne watched him whirl with her daughter's hand in his, she began to soften.

Out of breath the little ones sat on the floor. He quickly picked up his daughter and placed her at his waist, then reached for Brianna's hand. He began to escort her back to her mother, a tactic Julianne could not refuse.

"Fun, fun!" Brianna was shouting as she climbed onto her mother's lap.

"May I?" he asked, gesturing to an empty chair next to hers, and she consented. He paused, gathered himself, and sat down as he moved his daughter onto his knees. The two girls reached for each other and giggled together.

"You have a beautiful little one," he said in introduction. "And," he paused, "I think she has some pretty good moves."

"As do you," Julianne answered shyly with a grin.

"Hi, I'm Jason," he introduced himself enthusiastically extending a hand.

She accepted it and said, "Julianne. My friends call me Julie."

The girls were squirming again, demanding that their parents release them so that they could return to the dance floor.

"Do you know the groom?" he inquired.

"No, I'm here for the bride," she smiled and looked away.

"Oh, well, we need to get better acquainted then," he blurted and blushed. "I mean, well… the girls are great together. Maybe we should plan a play date for them?" he suggested and then worried if he had come on too strong.

Julianne just smiled and offered a nod as she looked away.

"Sorry," Jason said sincerely. "I don't mean to be imposing. But Kelsey's schedule is my sole responsibility."

Julianne's eyes widened.

"Well, I'm her only parent," he quietly offered in explanation.

Julianne began to nervously tap her foot on the floor.

"Sorry, again sorry," he seemed to be babbling now. "I've spoken out of turn. Sorry." And he waited for her to respond.

Julianne swallowed hard before she found her voice. "It's okay," she said calmly. "My daughter's name is Brianna," she offered it with a big smile. "They do seem to really like each other," she conceded. "Maybe a play date is a good idea," her tone suddenly became reconciliatory in nature. "I'm a single parent too," she admitted as their eyes met. "I understand."

"Oh," he was beginning to stammer, surprised at her confession. "Well, isn't that something… I mean, we have so much in common."

As their conversation continued, each keeping a watchful eye on the girls, Julianne's mood lightened and her guard came down. Soon the new couple was teasing about others on the dance floor and laughing together. They chatted for nearly an hour until Brianna returned to interrupt them. She was beginning to whine, obviously tired, and it was an hour past her bed time.

"We've got to be going," Julianne said as she began to gather her things hurriedly.

"Well, it was sure great to meet you," Jason replied, wondering if he should pose the question.

Then they spoke at the same time and Julianne smiled.

"I'm sorry, excuse me," Jason quickly inserted.

She paused and nodded.

"Well," he continued, "about that play date…" He paused as he reached into his jacket's vest pocket. "Can I give you my card?" he asked slyly. "No expectations," he noted, "but I hope you will call me," he smiled, "you know, for the girls' sake."

Julianne took the card, thanked him for sharing his daughter, and then turned, nearly running for the exit door.

Jason watched her go and sighed. "There goes your new Mommy," he whispered to Kelsey. "You know, when you know," he told himself and grinned with satisfaction.

CHAPTER ELEVEN

Julianne and Jason

The callback: that was especially hard for her. She'd look at his card and reach for the phone, then stop and toss it onto the countertop. Her mind reeled. Yes: he was nice. He was handsome. What harm could there be in getting to know him better?

No: it was too easy, too convenient, so it must be wrong. He could even be crazy. Maybe he was responsible for his wife's disappearance.

And the debate raged for days in her troubled mind. She studied the card closely. It was a business card. He apparently worked for Merkel Pharmaceuticals. Under his name was the word, "Developer." The card appeared to be professional enough. It was believable.

She held her breath as she dialed the telephone number on the card. A voicemail answered. She quickly hung up before it began recording a message.

Jason spent the next weeks watching the late show after rocking Kelsey to sleep, then wondered about Julianne. He couldn't get her out of his mind. She was beautiful. He liked her for being cautious. She must be smart. He longed to see her smile again.

He could kick himself. She apparently was not going to call. He should have been more assertive and asked for her number. He thought about contacting his friend, the groom. Surely this bride must know how to contact Julianne. But would she be scared off by such aggression? He reluctantly decided to wait a little longer.

Eventually he did get Aunt Betsy's number from his friend's wife and called for Julianne without hesitation. Betsy passed the phone to a surprised young woman whose voice was soft, even weak, her greeting full of cautious concern.

Later that week they met at a town park and pushed the girls on swings, side by side. Jason was very attentive to Brianna and caught her at the end of the slide. Julianne's heart began to open up as she watched

110

him run and chase after her daughter, both of them calling to the other and laughing hysterically.

Kelsey reached for Julianne's hand as they walked back to the parking lot. And just then the callous coating inside crumbled a little bit more.

Soon Jason was invited to Aunt Betsy's for dinner. Afterward, the host quickly escorted the two girls into a playroom full of toys and disappeared behind a closed door.

Jason and Julianne began to share their stories with each other. He married his childhood sweetheart right out of high school. They were poor and pregnant. His new bride, Pamela, insisted on having the baby at home. They lived in a basement apartment that was always damp and cold. Pam had been sick for several weeks before her labor pains began. She stayed in bed and ran a low grade fever, but she insisted that she did not need a doctor and refused to spend the money for one.

"It was probably an hour or two after the pains started that I became scared and called my mom. She came and I told her that I felt something was wrong. She told me to wait outside," Jason explained.

"Pamela's labor continued throughout the night. My mother gave me periodic updates and I could see that she was growing increasingly concerned. At daybreak she called for me. I picked up Pam and carried her to the car."

Jason caught his breath and held it in an attempt to hold back tears. He gathered his composure and continued.

"It was the blood that shocked me." And a sob came in a sudden outburst. Tears dropped from his face. Julianne reached for his hand.

"The sheets were soaked in blood," he continued. He paused and sobbed quietly as his body trembled.

Jason turned to face Julianne, his face wet, his eyes glossed over. "We rushed her to the emergency room. Kelsey arrived, but her mother, Pamela died eighteen hours later. They said it was from complications of childbirth."

Julianne felt his hand shaking and released it to hold him in a comforting embrace. The story touched her and tears came suddenly. It was something she had not experienced in many months, the simplicity of crying, venting freely, decompressing.

"Jason, I'm sorry, so... so sorry." She held him some more and felt his tremors recede. "It must have been terrible for you."

He pulled away and looked into her eyes, nodded, and began to sniffle.

"Wait," she said, "let me get you some tissues." When Julianne returned he had regained his composure and remained still in solemn silence.

Julianne handed him the box of tissues and sat close. She waited for a long minute and finally asked, "Are you alright?"

Jason was nodding and blowing his nose. He wiped at his eyes and sat still for another long moment.

"That's my story. That's how Kelsey lost her mom," and he paused. "What about you?" His eyes were searching for understanding.

Julianne stiffened at the direct question. She dropped her head and quickly considered the list of standard answers she frequently used. She chose the one about Brianna's father joining the army and not coming home. He was M.I.A.

112

"We weren't married," she confessed in a meager attempt to be somewhat truthful, but immediately felt submerged in shame. Her demeanor changed and the guilt of her lying was evident on her face.

Jason waited for more, but Julianne had become very quiet, seemed fidgety, and looked away.

"That's all?" he asked softly.

"Yeah, that's about it," her tone was nonchalant but she had become stoic and slightly agitated.

Each was isolated in that moment and needed relief from the pressure they felt. For Julianne it was remorse, as from recent times past, and she became aware of the breach of confidence she had just established. Suddenly she began to desire her daughter's company.

"Her bed time is soon," she finally suggested pleadingly.

"Oh yes, Kelsey's too," Jason answered with disappointment evident. "Thanks for the dinner," he paused, "guess I should be going."

Julianne agreed with a nod.

Determined not to let suspicions come into their new and budding relationship, Jason called the next day to again be thankful. They met that evening, again in the town park.

Jason and Julianne continued to see each other over the next months. Christmas was special, exchanging gifts, with even Brianna and Kelsey offering presents to each other. Jason showered the girls with dolls, toy cribs, and all the accessories required for them to be little mommies. Their determination to do so was both humorous and insightful at the same time.

Jason presented Julianne with an expensive tennis bracelet loaded with gemstones and diamond chips. She was a little reluctant to accept it but overjoyed at the same time.

She gave Jason a pair of leather driving gloves. The gift accompanied by the sparkle of her eyes, and a quick kiss under the mistletoe, was enough for him.

They continued to meet regularly and then began to date, getting a sitter for the girls. A romance was budding, and the physical attraction was something neither could deny, heating up, but held in restraint. Sometimes when alone in her bedroom after a romantic evening Julianne wondered why he was stalling. Jason was the perfect gentlemen, but the act was beginning to feel a little bit stale.

It was a beautiful late spring weekend, unseasonably warm as summer attempted its entry. Jason had planned a special outing and Julianne was asked to prepare a picnic lunch.

The state park was called "World's End," a name that seemed appropriate as Jason drove many miles down a dirt road, through uninhabited woodlands, along a creek. Finally, there was a sign for a picnic area. Jason turned right and quickly parked the car. The girls were anxious to get out, each holding a doll which they soon dropped as they began to explore nature's bounty.

"Don't let them get close to the stream," Julianne warned as she placed the picnic basket on the table.

"No worries," Jason returned with a smile. "I have a close watch on them."

Julianne had prepared fried chicken and homemade potato salad. She had orange creamsicle cake carefully boxed and candy treats ready for the girls. It was her birthday and although no announcement had been made about it, she suspected that Jason knew.

The red and white checkered cloth was clipped to the table and Julianne paused to take in the scene as she sat on the bench. Sunlight was beaming down through an opening in the trees above the stream, igniting young leaves in a bright green color, golden when tossed in the breeze. The brook was shallow with smooth rounded stones protruding above the water's surface, causing the customary babbling sound. Sunlight danced on the ripples of the water, crowning them with brilliance. Jason was standing there, looking into the stream, his reflection evident to her. She blinked and sighed. Peace was prominent in this place as God's creation was manifested with beauty. It was beginning to settle in.

Kelsey was approaching her father and Brianna sat in a mossy patch on the other side of the picnic table. Julianne turned toward her daughter and heard a strange sound. It was the snarling of a wild animal. She stood quickly.

"Jason!"

He heard the panic in her voice and spun around. He saw Brianna, a twig in her hand, facing an animal that growled at her. It appeared to be a medium sized dog. Slowly, it came closer to her. The intensity of its growling increased. It snarled and displayed its canine teeth, long and pointed, located behind its incisors as its gums vibrated in white foam.

Brianna was in danger. Julianne ran to her. As she bent over to lift Brianna the creature crouched and readied to pounce on them.

115

Jason lunged, coming between it and Brianna, shielding her and Julianne form its attack. It jumped and bit into Jason's forearm, his right side. Its grip was firm. Jason sprung back and the canine went with him, unwilling to release its hold. He fell to a sitting position.

Julianne grabbed Brianna and ran back toward the stream. Halfway there she met Kelsey who was coming to see about the commotion. Julianne took hold of her upper arm and ushered her to the car, the little girl partly running and dragging her feet. She shoved the girls in through the driver's door, the closest to them, and jumped inside, quickly slamming it shut.

Jason and the wild animal where spinning and rolling on the ground. She could hear his screams, then cursing. It was still growling and then it yelped with a shrill scream. Jason was pounding it in the face with his left fist. It finally released its hold and retreated into a thick bush.

Jason was stunned. He could hear it still growling and snarling from the nearby thicket. As he stood he saw a pool of blood on the ground. It was dripping from his arm and streaming down his palm and fingers, squirting from there. He looked for Julianne and the girls.

She was observing all this from the front seat of the car. Seeing his confusion, she hit the horn button. The creature retreated further, back into the woods. Jason limped as he ran for the safety of the car.

He dropped into the driver's seat and closed the door. Panic was still written on his face.

"What the hell was that?" Julianne screamed. The girls in the back seat began crying.

116

Jason groaned and pushed on the back of the seat as he attempted to raise his arm. Blood was oozing out of the many puncture wounds, dripping onto his pants. He was trembling, attempting to release the final surge of adrenaline.

"Here," Julianne instructed as she began to rustle through a bag that was on the car's floor, near her feet. She had brought a towel in case the girl's stepped into the stream. "Wrap your arm in this."

She watched in horror as he attempted to follow her instruction, restricted by the steering wheel and the use of one hand. "Let me," she informed. She placed the edge of the towel on top, draped it over, and turned his arm to see the underside. It was punctured and torn.

"We have to get you to the hospital," she said. He was hitting at his pockets with his left hand, searching for the car keys.

"Can you drive?" she asked, not really wanting to assume the duty.

"My keys are in my pants pocket, right side," he instructed, "can you reach them?" He stretched his leg, pushed back on the seat, and raised his injured arm.

Cautiously, she reached into his pocket while trying to dodge the injured limb. She pushed further in. "I got 'em," she noted with relief.

"Give them to me. I want to get us out of her," he instructed, "to a safe place. Then we can change positions. I need you to drive," he admitted, "I'm feeling a little bit light headed."

"Okay… okay, let's go!" She placed the keys in the ignition and started the car.

Jason threw the shifter into reverse and stomped on the accelerator, spinning the car's rear wheels. It jerked wildly as he attempted to back out of the lane. He hit the brake pedal and the car spun, nearly crashing into a tree. The road was clear ahead and he seemed to gain control as he went forward. Julianne looked back, wanting to see the wild animal once again, but it had disappeared. The car swerved.

"Keep your focus," she instructed. "Just a little further and we can switch places." She looked at Jason. His eyes were glossing over. Beads of sweat hung on his brow. He gripped the wheel firmly with both hands. His head bobbed and the car swerved again.

"Honey," she said with affection, "you got this, just a little bit further." She began to realize his act of heroism. "Thank you," she whispered, "thank you for saving us."

He turned her way. "Are you okay? Are the girls okay?"

"Yes, we're fine," she reported. "You saved us from that wild beast."

He nodded and over steered, causing the car to sway. "It's okay," she said in a soothing tone, and then, "I love you."

The words were unexpected and Julianne surprised herself in hearing them vocalized. "You saved us," she repeated, her mind still in a whirl. "You're our hero."

The road widened and Jason brought the car to a sudden stop. They changed places quickly. He fastened his seat belt, groaned, and leaned his head against the door's window.

Julianne felt the pressure, the responsibility she then assumed. She got the car moving again. "Oh my god," she mumbled, "I don't know where I'm going."

"Straight," Jason answered unexpectedly, "get to the main road, then turn left. I think that will get us to the closest town." He paused and drew in a long breath. "Then stop and call for help."

Near silence: there was only the sound of the hum of the engine, air whistling at the windows, the whine of the tires on the road, and shallow breathing. She looked in the rearview mirror. The girls, leaning against each other, had fallen asleep. A large cloud of dust formed behind the car.

"God help us," she prayed quietly. The next ten minutes seemed like an hour. She looked at Jason. His eyes were closed. "I love you," she whispered again.

CHAPTER TWELVE

Julianne took the girls into the waiting room adjacent to the emergency ward. It was crowded. Others slumped in their chairs and coughed. A teenage boy extended his leg after limping to and falling into a padded chair. His shoe and sock were removed and she could see that his ankle was swollen. She scanned the room for a remote spot, isolated from the others. She feared what germs may be airborne there.

The receptionist had promised to call Jason's mother. Julianne checked the time. The girls were already beginning to squirm. She looked for a storybook to share with them.

Finally, the door opened and Jason's mother came running in. She looked wildly at Julianne. "Is he okay?" she asked. "Where is my son?"

Julianne took her hand. "He's going to be fine. The doctor said his wounds are only superficial."

"Oh, thank God!" she shouted. "Can I see him?"

"The receptionist's office is just around that corner," she instructed as she pointed in that direction.

The woman paused. "Thank you, Julianne," she offered. "I'm sorry for being so abrupt," she paused. "I'm just glad you weren't hurt."

"It was Jason," she said as her eyes filled again with tears. "He saved us."

"Oh yes, my little solider!" she remembered. "Well, I must go to see him now. Thank you."

Twenty minutes later she returned. "He's going to be okay," she affirmed to Julianne, "but the doctor said he will have to get the rabies shots."

"Oh no," Julianne exclaimed, "Is that serious?"

"No, he'll manage it okay," Jason's mother reasoned. "Thank God that is all. But what was it that attacked you in those woods?" she inquired.

"I don't know," Julianne saw the animal again, etched in her memory by her mind's eye. "It looked like a wild dog."

"They think it was a coyote," she informed, "sick with the disease."

"Oh," she stammered, "that's even scarier."

The grandmother offered to take the girls home. "You stay here, honey," she noted, "Jason wants to see you soon."

"Sure, I'll wait.'

"Well then, come on girls," she directed. "We have lots to do, you know."

Julianne smiled to herself as she watched them leaving the hospital.

Jason was sedated and admitted for observation. A few hours later, Julianne took his car and returned to her home. She would call him in the morning.

He was released the next day and then disappeared for the next three. Julianne was beginning to become concerned when he did not immediately return her phone calls.

It was the Wednesday after the attack that Jason stood on her doorstep, a bouquet of flowers in his left hand. His right arm was held securely in a sling.

She was surprised to see him standing there when she opened the door and threw her arms around him. He winced when she bumped, then squeezed his elbow.

"Oh, I'm so sorry," she greeted him, realizing her mistake.

"I'm happy to see you again," he replied.

"Please, come in. I've been worried about you," she admitted.

They went into the front parlor and sat next to each other on the sofa.

"Jason, I want to thank you," she paused, "I was thinking about what you did."

"What do you mean?" he asked.

"Well, it was the way you ran to save us. You went after that wild beast. You didn't hesitate, not even for a fraction of a second. If you had..." her voice drifted off.

"Julianne, I won't let anything or anyone hurt you or Brianna," he affirmed. "You're my girls."

"Yes, but…" she hesitated, "you don't really know us." She looked into his eyes. "There's so much that I haven't told you yet."

"I knew that you'd tell me when you're ready," he said.

"But you don't even know who her father is," Julianne complained. "What if he is a mad man, or mentally ill?"

The question stunned Jason who thought momentarily before answering. "It doesn't matter," he said firmly.

"It does… or it might," she reiterated. "How can you be so sure?"

"Well, something that you don't know about me is that I was adopted." He looked to see her surprise. "My birth mom was an addict and a homeless person. I lived in foster care homes until I was four years old and then my parents adopted me."

"What happened to your real mom?" Julianne asked shyly.

"You mean my birth mom?" Jason corrected. "You have met my real mom."

"Yes… sorry, that's what I meant."

"We don't know," Jason answered. "Really, it doesn't matter," and he paused. "I doubt that she is still alive, that she survived her lifestyle."

Julianne looked surprised.

"You see," Jason continued, "my parents had to face the same struggle you now have. My pediatrician always told them that genetics was not nearly as strong of an influence as environment. They truly loved me, cared for me, and helped me become who and what I am today," he said with pride. "That's all that matters!"

"Wow," Julianne responded. "I had no idea."

"You see," Jason continued, "God brought us together to redeem our lives, to save us from our hurtful past. And we make the perfect family."

Julianne smiled as she became teary eyed.

"Adoption is His thing, and my thing too," Jason declared. "You and I, both of us, we have been adopted into the family of the King Most High. You are His princess."

Tears fell from her face.

"I am His... and your prince," Jason offered. "And I want to adopt Brianna. I want to be her father. And I want to marry you, Julianne. I love you very much!"

"Oh Jason!" She threw her arms around him and held him close for a long minute. Looking into his eyes she whispered, "I love you too."

The next afternoon they met at the park without the girls in tow. They needed to talk some more.

She took his hand and led him to a bench. "Now I have to tell you all of it. You have to know."

"Okay," he answered with wonder in his eyes.

While holding his hand Julianne told Jason everything: she described her father, the farm at Sweetened Vales with Frank and Emma, her first boyfriend Vincent, and his jealous rival Barton. She continued with what happened on that day in July nearly four years ago and how it affected her.

Jason listened intently without making any interruptions. When she finished she was crying softly.

"I have just one question," he noted in response.

"Oh yes," Julianne teased. "I imagine that you will have many more after today," then flashed a half smile.

"My question, my sweetheart, is simply this," and he paused, "will you marry me?"

Joy came upon her with laughter and she choked on it at first. She turned her face upward to him and it was beaming with love. Her eyes glowed and the smile she wore was brighter than any before.

Her heart was healed.

"Yes, yes! I do!" she shouted.

The couple embraced and kissed passionately. Then, arm in arm, they began their walk; it was the beginning of their new life, their journey together. He held his head high, a smile continuous upon his face. With every few steps she looked to him. Inside she was overjoyed. They went a little further when she stopped suddenly and squeezed his hand.

"Honey," she addressed him with new found affection. "There's one more thing I have to do," and she paused. "I have to meet with Vincent. I need to close that chapter," she explained, "I need to be sure he understands."

"Sure," Jason replied. "I understand." And his smile persisted.

CHAPTER THIRTEEN

Julianne finally calls Vincent...

It was a balmy day in July when Vincent received the call from Julianne. He was watching TV that evening with a fan blowing nearby when he heard the phone ring. He had not heard from her those last four years. A rapidly maturing young man, he was anxious to get on with his life. He had just earned his Bachelor's degree in Biology and was presently completing his registration to pursue graduate school; a Master's Degree in Botany was within view.

The phone persisted to ring. Subconsciously he was counting them. Eleven, twelve, and thirteen: "Okay, I'm coming," he mumbled, deciding the call must be important. It interrupted his favorite show, Hawaii Five-O, but he could already guess who had committed the crime.

A small framed picture sat on his desk near the phone. It was the work crew at Sweetened Vales. Pops stood near the center, Bart to his left, and Vincent to his right with Julianne standing erect next to him. Pops wore that wide brimmed straw hat he was noted for. Bart sported a sleeveless muscle shirt. Vincent didn't like his image – his hair was matted in sweat and his cut-off denim shorts were too short to look natural. The only person smiling was Julianne, her eyes glowing from a dark complexion, a deep bronze tan, her long curly red hair was pulled to her left side, framing her face as it tussled under her chin and covered her chest. In times past Vincent had studied every detail of the photograph, longing for more of her.

"Hello," he answered weakly, feeling little interest in the call while still gazing at the TV, concentrating there.

"Vincent, how are you doing?" It was not the question, but the voice he heard that stunned him.

His mind began to spin. All of a sudden, he experienced a rush of adrenaline followed by a feeling of dread. He needed to verify that it really was her and wondered why she would be calling now.

"Julianne?" he asked for affirmation as his voice stammered.

"Hey," she answered in a tone that teased. "Are you still the fastest strawberry picker in Pennsylvania?" she asked, immediately reminding him of their shared past.

There was an awkward silence.

Vincent's mind was racing. His emotions were raw. Memories came flooding in.

"Vince," she interrupted, "are you still there?"

"Yeah," he spoke from a distant place, a time long ago.

"How are your grandparents?" Julianne asked. "I sure miss them," she confessed, "Frank and Emma are such good people," she asserted. "Even better than I knew."

Vincent wondered at the way she qualified the compliment. Sweetened Vales, that very special place and the key players that dominated his impressionable high school years, it all came flooding back upon him with a rush in a smothering swell. He gasped for air in the memory tsunami.

"Pops and Granny are good," Vincent offered no specific information, still wondering at the purpose of Julie's call and her sudden interruption of his life. He had finally found his place without her and felt as though he landed on his feet again. His recovery after her disappearance and continued absence took several years. Now, at the hearing of her voice once again, Vincent felt his solid ground begin to shake. This earthquake could cause all that he had gained, his plans for the future, present goals and purpose, to come crashing down.

"Julie," Vincent found clarity of thought, "How are you doing?"

"I'm good," she shot back quickly and paused. "How about you?"

"Fine, just fine," Vincent answered. Each was testing and sensing the temperature of the conversation before jumping in. Each was still uncertain of the other.

He waited for her to speak. There was another awkward silence.

"I'm finally healed," she reluctantly offered. She had planned her call, scripted and rehearsed it, but suddenly those intended words seemed inappropriate.

They stung at Vincent as she immediately raised the issue that bothered him most. He was annoyed by the questions that remained unanswered still: What was her illness? Why was she hospitalized? Where did she go?

He simply did not know what to say next and words evaded him.

"I always marveled at the healings at Sweetened Vales," Julianne continued as she realized that her previous statement was too personal. "I really miss that place," she offered in reconciliation.

It was another mystery he had subjected to the recesses of his mind. That vault opened just then and confronted him with sequestered memories and the questions they imposed.

128

Their telephone conversation ended with an invitation, a suggestion to meet at a local restaurant, a chain that was past its heyday, offering an inexpensive lunch special to the few who still patronized the establishment. It would be quiet there, a private place, a good place to talk. Despite feeling hugely curious, Vincent was cold hearted; the pain of rejection he felt had never been completely erased. Reluctantly, he agreed.

Vincent scanned the parking lot as he pulled in that Wednesday at 1 PM promptly. He wouldn't know her car, but he might recognize her. After all, it had been many years since they had been together. The lobby was vacant so he stood near the sign that read, "Please Wait To Be Seated." It seemed like an hour, but in reality it was about ten minutes until a disheveled looking middle-aged man appeared. "Just one?" he asked in monotone.

"Well," Vincent cleared his throat, "actually I'm meeting a young woman. Is there a chance she has already arrived?" he asked.

"No, I don't believe so," the hostess who would also be his server announced. "I haven't seen any singles."

Vincent nodded in recognition.

"Please come this way," the man instructed as he reached for the menu folder. He escorted him to a booth at a large window that afforded a view of the parking area.

"Will this suit?" he asked bluntly.

"Sure. Yes, this is okay," Vincent answered. "Will you watch for my lady friend?" he asked with instruction.

"But of course," he replied, quickly spun on his heels and headed for the kitchen.

Vincent was beginning to feel uncomfortable and questioned himself on the wisdom of the meeting. He nearly had himself convinced to leave when a sedan pulled into the parking lot and stopped near his car. The door opened. He saw a foot reach for the ground. She wore a high heeled slip-on. The ankle was thin, the lower leg slender with a muscular calf. Then there was a second foot and the woman that emerged was gorgeous.

He gasped. Her hair was floating back from her face as it lifted on a gentle breeze.

To describe her with one word, she was cheerful. She smiled constantly, always spoke with sincerity, and somehow broke through the façade strangers felt, quickly touching their hearts. She did not waste words or seconds. Her presence was demanding, and an inner beauty and energy radiated from her.

And, she was beautiful. Her hair was long, thick and wavy, reddish orange - vermillion in color. Her eyes were large and green. Her cheekbones, slightly elevated, centered the perfect nose above thick lips that formed Cupid's bow. Her smile was wide, her teeth glowed in a perfect row, and it all combined to be genuinely sweet, and vastly appealing.

Vincent felt suddenly overheated and perspiration formed on his forehead as the man appeared again too soon. He had not yet gained his composure. The hostess extended his hand toward Vincent. Looking at her he asked, "Miss, is this the young man you were to meet?"

She ignored the question and rushed past him to Vince who stood just in time to receive her embrace. He held his arms outstretched but then as the hug endured, he bent them at the elbows and felt the small of her back.

"Vince, you look great!" she touted a wide smile.

"As do you," his enthusiasm was squelched by a lack of confidence.

She took his hands in hers and looked into his eyes. Time stopped just then, until Vincent spoke softly. "Shall we sit," he said awkwardly and motioned toward the booth.

They shared the required niceties. She was doing well, rebuilding her life at last. He was in school, pursuing his graduate degree. His field sounded very promising.

"Thanks for agreeing to meet," she finally became focused on the purpose of their gathering. "It was a long road for me, Vince. I had a tough time."

The comment grated him. What about all that he endured? Inside, Vincent felt like a ping pong ball knocked off the table and bouncing off the walls of the small room where the contest was held. Defensively, he was challenged for the isolation, the rejection, and the uncertainty he felt for many years… and the pain it caused. He was still hurting over the fact that no one cared enough to tell him the truth about what had happened to her, including her.

Vincent was overcome by emotion and ready to speak when the server interrupted them. It was an awkward few moments as they placed their order. He insisted that she go first. Finally, after much consideration she ordered a half salad and a cup of soup. Vincent ordered a BLT and fries.

He seemed calm, but when he knew he must speak again, he felt anger surge within because of the selfishness she had unintentionally expressed.

"Are you still just focused on yourself? Why have you bothered to contact me now?" he blurted.

"I was traumatized," Julianne answered defensively. "It was more than I could handle. In the hospital for the mentally ill, I was in danger of being abused in many ways. When Brianna came, I was consumed with the newborn baby."

It was all news to him but the revelation that stuck in his brain came with the word 'baby.' He assumed that she had wed. "Well," Vincent reasoned, "at one point you got better and began a relationship. When did you get married?"

"Jason pursued me," she noted defensively as her enthusiasm waned. "He came at me fast and he was very determined," Julianne swallowed hard and continued, "He wasn't deterred by the baby. He literally swept me off my feet." She looked away briefly as her mind spun dizzily. "We're not married, not yet," she corrected him. "Our wedding is set for next May. But this isn't about him. Vince, I have always cared about you."

"But why now," he demanded as his tone softened. "You have moved on. You're as good as married with children. Aren't you happy?"

132

Secretly he wondered if he still had a chance of winning her back, but then again, felt rejection. It was the fact he had to acknowledge. She never really gave him a chance.

"Vincent," she addressed him firmly. "Did you ever know what happened?" She looked into his eyes, "Even so, there is more and you cannot know unless I tell you."

"Well, I don't think it matters," he was still feeling the hurt of losing her to begin with.

"We need to close that chapter of our lives," she reasoned. "I need to…" her voice was firm as she looked steely into his eyes. "You need to close it too Vince," she suggested.

He quickly looked away. There was a young family sitting at a nearby table and the noise of their kids drew his attention to them. A little boy about six years old was breaking crayons into small pieces and throwing them at his sister who sat across the table, a space intended to keep them from fighting, but they were yelling at each other. The little girl, about three years younger, was scribbling vigorously while continuing off the placemat and writing on the table. Vincent looked to their parents expecting to see them correct the misbehavior. The young couple, both nicely dressed, was looking at their smart phones, not speaking and not showing any regard for their children.

"Bart disappeared," Julie demanded his attention, "but we found him."

"I heard rumors," Vincent admitted as he returned his attention to his guest. "But really, I don't know what happened to him," he paused to contain his emotions, "and I really don't care."

"I got letters from him before he was killed." The words stung at her reluctant listener. She had finally captured his full attention. "And did you know that it was your grandfather who saved me?"

Vincent was stunned at the assertion.

"There are some things that we need to clear up. I want to be free from the past," she noted firmly. "Don't you feel the same way?" She looked deep into his eyes and saw uncertainty there. More than that, she perceived that he was still held in bondage by the events that occurred during the summers they shared, many years earlier.

As their discussion continued, her comments served as the introduction of facts unknown to Vincent, information that had been concealed in his past. Now, she was determined that he should know it all. She began to unpack many hidden secrets to him.

CHAPTER FOURTEEN

What happened to them: Julianne, Barton, and Vincent...

In telling her story, Julianne began with the most traumatic of events. She was feeling defensive and Vincent needed to understand that she had little to no control of what occurred then.

How she became ill, and why she was hospitalized, Vincent needed to understand it all.

"When I discovered that I was pregnant, I lost myself," she confessed. "Then, I was in real danger once they placed me in a hospital for the mentally ill."

And he wondered what happened to her there.

#

Initially, she had spent three days in the local hospital due to the injuries she sustained from the kidnapping and assault, but the description of that event came later in their conversation.

Julianne was released to go home, but then soon returned as she became agitated, most likely having a nervous breakdown. The trigger for this behavior was when her doctor verified her pregnancy with a blood test.

She was admitted to the ward designated for the mentally disturbed. Despite the regiment of a large dosage of medication, mostly sedatives, she made little progress in returning to plausible reality during the next five days. She was stoic, refused to talk, stared off somewhere into a distant place, wept frequently, and on occasion, had a verbal outburst, repeating phrases of vulgarity that was not directed at any specific person. The anger she felt was consuming, and uncontrollable. Several times she tried to break loose of her restraints and once cut her wrist deeply during the attempt. It was obvious she intended to escape.

She had great anxiety with high blood pressure, tense muscles, clammy hands, dizziness, upset stomach, and frequent trembling and shaking. Hank observed all these symptoms to be increasing as she also suffered with insomnia. Then the hallucinations began, with extreme mood swings and unexplained fear.

Additional medications were prescribed during the two weeks she stayed there and finally, she seemed to be calming down, so they sent her home again. Within three days, she attempted suicide, taking an overdose of sleeping pills. Her father intervened just in time to save her life. That was when she was hospitalized yet again, for the third time, but this time her stay would be short, due to a transfer ordered by her doctor.

Upon reexamination, her physician ordered placement at Haven of Hope Hospital for the Mentally Ill. Julianne's father, her legal guardian, strongly objected. The reputation of the place was well known. Allegations of sexual abuse were rampant. It seemed that few who were admitted became well again. Mental patients had a hopeless plight, were held in captivity for many years, and most never returned to their families.

"There are few alternatives," Doc Evans replied with dismay. "We can't keep her in the hospital any longer, and you can't manage her at home to keep her safe. She needs a treatment plan to become well again."

Hank had to agree in principle but because of the alleged abuses, could not accept Haven to be a viable treatment option. After all, Julianne had suffered a nervous breakdown, was disturbed, but not hopelessly ill. "But what about a private practice psychiatrist?" he asked. "Can't they help?"

"Sure," the doctor agreed. "And that might be better for her, but they are very expensive," and he paused to wait for confirmation.

Hank looked to the floor, knowing that he could not afford such care, and suddenly felt ashamed of his failure to give his daughter the very best.

"I can make a recommendation," Doctor Evans suggested. "But she needs professional care and supervision. A qualified person has to be responsible for her," he explained. "I'll give you until tomorrow morning to make your decision."

It was late the next day that Hank kissed his daughter gently on the forehead and placed her hand at her side. She remained silent and motionless. "I'm sorry, Honey," he choked as tears welled in his eyes. "I'm not giving up on you... so, so sorry."

A tear drop splattered onto her face.

"I'll see you soon." He stepped back as a nurse directed two men with a gurney into the small room.

Hank watched in horror as they pushed his daughter, a beautiful young woman who less than a month ago was full of vitality and loved life, down the long hallway. Now she was only an empty shell. The lights blinked and he wept quietly unable to keep his shoulders from shaking, but trying to conceal the overwhelming grief he felt. He coughed, turned and limped away, headed in the opposite direction toward the parking garage.

The ambulance that transported Julianne was a '67 Cadillac station wagon with a raised roof, red and white in color. There was only enough interior room for one collapsed gurney, leaving a small place for a medic to sit alongside the patient. The siren remained silent. Hope for Julianne was fading like the sunset as it gave way to the impending darkness of a black night.

Hank sat in the rocker in front of the kitchen. He was staring with a blank look on his face, looking toward the street, but wasn't actually seeing anything. Loneliness penetrated the house that recently was filled with enthusiasm and laughter resulting from the sometimes foolish but most often kind and generous antics of his loving daughter, Julianne. Her incarceration felt like death. His heart ached. The scene in the hospital, his weak promise, her non-response, their taking her away: it all replayed in his mind like a bad dream, one that could not be shaken, and not confined to slumber.

He was drowsy after a stressful day and his mind raced toward exhaustion. He recalled his cold-hearted demeanor and regretted not embracing Julianne before she was carted away. He had not expressed his affection for her. Now, not knowing when he would see her again, he began to cry.

Questions that condemned continued to crash into his weakening mind. He wondered what to do next, how to pay for a private doctor so he could get her out of the mental hospital, and where to get the money it would cost. He considered the self assertion of being a worthless failure, and again heard the accusation of his wife long passed away. He believed she would have done better. He had let everyone down.

But it was at his lowest, at that very moment, that he decided to do three things. First, he talked to God. His prayer was whispered from his troubled mind that began to find clarity only in decisive action.

"Oh God, why did this have to happen to us?" he asked as a tear escaped the confinement of his eye's lid.

"Please be with her now. Please protect her from the evil that lurkes there. Please show me how to help her. Oh God, I beg you, please help us now."

Next, he picked up the phone to call Frank, his neighbor and good friend. Emma answered and explained that her husband had gone out to the barn to check something before turning in, but could be anywhere on the farm by now.

"How is Julianne doing?" she asked and continued, "such a sweet girl. I am praying for her and trusting that she will receive the best of care in the hospital."

"She's not there," Hank blurted, "Not anymore."

Emma gasped.

"They took her to Haven," he continued. "My gawd, anywhere but there," he lamented.

"Oh no, not there," Emma's voice trembled slightly. "There must be something else they can do."

"Only a private doctor, a shrink," Hank answered curtly. "But Emma, I don't have the money," he complained.

"Do it anyway," she instructed without hesitation. "Do it Hank, call the doctor," she ordered firmly, "and do it now."

And he nodded to himself just having received the confirmation for the third thing on his 'to do' list. "Thanks Emma. I just needed to hear someone say it. I will call. And please, have Frank stop by when he can."

"Of course, but of course he will," Emma confirmed. "Don't despair, keep hoping..." she paused, "and please, keep us informed."

"Will do," he said as he placed his finger on the button in the cradle of the telephone's handset to conclude the call.

Hank reached into his shirt pocket and found the slip of paper used for writing prescriptions on which Doctor Evans made a recommendation. He carefully placed it on the table near the telephone. He intended to dial the number jotted there, the first thing the next morning, to contact Doctor Charles Chamberlin, MD/Psychiatrist.

At the Haven of Hope Hospital for the Mentally Ill, Earl James was stuck in a job that was going nowhere. In his prime, 39 years of age and in perfect health, but with a few extra pounds hanging on his waist line, he served as deputy director of admissions, knowing he had reached the top of the ladder. To receive such a cushy job, administrators at "Haven," as it was called, had to have some political clout to be appointed by the Governor's office.

James lived a quiet life in a small town with his wife of twelve years and two daughters, both in elementary school. Jeannie, their mother, was a typical housewife, active in the PTA and hosted her bridge club once every two months. These women were independent, privately complained about their husbands and no longer considered their appearance to be a priority. Looking good was something their men were no longer worthy of; there were other indulgences they now preferred and granted to themselves.

The drudgery of his life continued at home. The spark of romance in his marriage had long ago been extinguished. Earl sought physical pleasure elsewhere and followed the lead of his predecessors who worked at Haven, for "comfort," to intimately know female patients there. He had the advantage and maintained seniority when it came to whom he would have exclusively. It was in his job description to familiarize himself with the files of incoming patients and to review their placement. When an attractive female arrived, he would soon become better acquainted by scheduling a personal and often intimate, interview.

He looked at Julianne's photo attached to the Patient Record with a paper clip and observed her to be very attractive. The file indicated her age, recently turned eighteen, and that she was pregnant. Earl considered her to be a perfect candidate for an extra-marital affair.

His small office was located in the east wing, adjacent to a foyer nearest to the small parking area at the entrance of the facility. A receptionist who answered the telephone there had an intercom connected to several tiny offices like his and provided secretarial duties to the lower-level executives who shared her duty roster.

"Yes, Mister James," Susan answered reluctantly. "How can I help you?" she inquired.

"There is a new patient," he began, "Miss Culp, Julianne Culp," he clarified her name. "Arrived late yesterday, I believe," he intended to sound authoritative.

"Yes," she interrupted, "I know the one." Her mind began racing as she became suspicious of his intention.

"Please schedule an induction interview," he instructed firmly, "I want to see her as soon as possible," he stated firmly.

"Yes sir," she responded as she had nearly a hundred times before. But this time she could feel her blood pressure rising. Thinking quickly, she asked, "Should I inform her attending doctor of the meeting also," she paused, hoping for a way to make the closed-door session less private. "I'm sure he should be included in the interview," she suggested.

"No... no, that won't be necessary at this time," he tried to sound resolutely calm as if he was following proper procedure.

"Then her nurse?" Susan shot back with the suggestion quickly.

"No!" Earl spoke louder as he tried to contain his anger.

"Yes sir," she spoke in monotone. She pushed the intercom button to disconnect and hit the top of the desk with her fist as she considered blowing the whistle on her boss. She intentionally scheduled his visit with "Miss Julie" as far ahead on the calendar as possible.

#

As she turned her head her vision blurred. Voices echoed as if in a distant place, a cavern of confusion. Julianne slowly shuffled her feet encased in cloth envelopes, stumbling on the cracked concrete. The patient couldn't perceive what was happening to her. She didn't know where she was.

Julianne had been escorted into a large room with small windows on one side. It was a ground level hallway that was mostly vacant, dimly lit by a few wall-mounted bulbs of low wattage that glowed from behind wire cages.

142

She saw a bug emerge from the wider crevice in the floor. Suddenly it was enlarged to become a giant monster insect that reeled up on its hind feet with tentacles reaching toward her. She screamed as the cockroach scampered away toward the wall and concealed itself in another crack there.

Occasionally a nurse passed by quickly, hurrying to her next assignment, but patients lingered there.

Today the room was dark, as heavy clouds hung low in the sky outside. It appeared that a storm may be approaching. The hallway that connected two wings of the old institution was cold and damp. Dirty.

Julianne's attention was drawn to another woman with long gray hair, matted at the back of her head. She was stomping her feet: one, then the other, back and forth, and mumbling all the while. As she approached, the woman turned to her with wide eyes and shouted, "Away you witch. He is coming. He is coming soon."

Gussie Russett saw the frightened look on Julianne's face. "I am having a baby... Satan's son!" she proclaimed and smiled with an evil grin. It was her delusion, but a swelled abdomen gave the appearance of one who was expecting. Perhaps she was – who would know?

Others who looked similar, they actually were with child. The unfortunate act was said to have been caused by male patients who managed to open locked doors in the middle of the night.

Officially, Haven was taking extreme measures to guarantee the privacy and safety of its female residents. Unofficially, and hidden away from public view, was a large closet at the rear of the female ward. It contained a rocking chair and a baby's bassinette. The makeshift nursery was used only until Child Protective Services came, but if the illegitimate

143

child was born on a federal holiday, it might be more than forty-eight hours until they arrived.

Julianne was in grave danger in that horrible place. The stage was set for her abuse, torture, and demise into long lasting insanity. But somehow, she was suddenly rescued, thank God, for she may have been lost forever. But how?

CHAPTER FIFTEEN

Julianne continued to tell Vincent about her bewildering past, hoping to achieve resolution and a peace with him, which she sorely needed as she prepared for a new beginning, the next chapter in her life.

"Vince, it was really a rough time for me. I crashed, and my father was unable to help me. I think he was ashamed and decided to keep my condition a secret."

"I was like a child lost in a crowd. It was smothering; people pressing in from all sides, everyone rushing about, but no one pausing long enough to hear me, or show that they cared. Even in silence, that which was primarily induced by the medications, I was shouting for help. I panicked!"

"It was Bart... you knew that he hurt me... didn't you?" She saw his blank expression. "That's why we both disappeared the same day."

And Vincent wondered how it would feel to be abandoned in your time of greatest need, unable to help yourself, and completely vulnerable. He had suspected his rival, but was anxious to learn the details of Bart's alleged assault. He had always wondered if Julianne was complicit in their affair. Some people said she was too flirtatious, encouraged it, even deserved it. Others described it as a crime, but then became mum when pressed for details.

#

It was Sunday, mid-day when she managed to return home after the assault, stumbling onto the rear porch, her mind spinning; a loud buzzing noise was rattling in her ears. Her skull throbbed as her brain cried in pain. Blood oozed out of her head and continued to trickle down the back of her neck, flowing into the crevice formed by her spine. She tripped on the top step to the porch and fell, head long, onto the wooden floor.

"Papa," her voice was weak. "Please help me," she pleaded. "I need help."

Hank heard a noise at the rear of the house. He was standing at the kitchen sink peeling potatoes and dropped everything when he thought he also heard Julianne's voice.

Earlier that morning he called the state police when she could not be found in the house. A missing person's report would not be filed until she was absent for forty-eight hours. He didn't know what else to do, so he busied himself with household chores as he watched, peering out the windows, desperately hoping for her safe return.

He pulled back the curtain on the rear door window and peeked outside. There was a body lying there on the floor of the porch. He threw the door open.

"Julie!" he shouted, "Is that you?" But he already knew the answer. He rolled her onto her back, cradling her head in the palm of his hand. She opened her eyes half way.

"Papa," she whispered as she recognized her father, affirming her rescue just before she fainted. She was going into shock.

Hank felt something on his hand and gently placed her head back onto the floor. Her eyes were closed.

His hand was covered in blood, sticky to the touch. He felt panic rising. He jumped to his feet, ran back into the kitchen toward the sitting area and reached for the telephone. He fumbled through some envelopes there. He knew that he saved the seven-digit number, the one for the local volunteer ambulance service. His hand shook as he lifted the receiver.

It seemed like hours until he could hear the faint wailing of the siren, but in reality, it was just about thirty minutes. Julianne had come back around and sat on the floor, leaning against a porch post. Her breathing was shallow and rapid. She was sweating profusely and complained of thirst. Hank quickly fetched a large glass of water.

"You're going to be okay," he urged, hoping to bring comfort to his injured daughter. "They're coming. Help is on its way. Please, please try to relax."

She swallowed a couple gulps of water and handed the glass back to him. "It was Bart," she said in a volume that was nearly inaudible.

Hank leaned in closer, not sure of what he heard. "What did you say?" he asked.

"Bart. It was Bart!" she nearly shouted back at him. "He, he…" and she began to whimper.

"What did he do?" Hank persisted. "What did he do to you?"

"He kidnapped me," she managed and coughed.

It was then that Hank noticed her top open, several of its buttons missing. She had been holding it closed.

"He tried to rape me," she blurted and began to cry.

In the waiting room the second hand moved in slow motion, each of its huge leaps resounding in his brain with a crash. Time paused as Hank fidgeted with his pocket watch and chain. Finally, a man in scrubs stepped through the doorway and asked if a relative of Julianne Culp was present. Hank stumbled as he rose, his numb leg faltering under his weight.

"She's going to be okay," he announced, "but I think she should stay the night for observation."

Hank looked puzzled and concerned at the same time. "What's wrong with her?" he asked.

"She has a nasty cut, a gash on the back of her head and a mild concussion. We dressed it and closed it up," he paused, "twelve stitches."

"She has lost some blood," he continued, "so we want to watch her to see if she will need a transfusion," the doctor elaborated. "We're checking her blood type. Do you know it?"

"Sure, she can stay," Hank consented while ignoring the second question.

"And there's one more thing," the physician noted. "I think she should be examined for sexual assault."

Hank frowned and clenched his fists.

"Do you know if she was active?" the doctor asked.

"If you're asking if she had a boyfriend," Hank corrected, "well, the answer is no! She was almost always home, with me."

"Yes, okay, Mister Culp," he answered defensively. "A woman nurse will conduct the exam. She knows how to be discrete. Don't worry, we will take good care of your daughter," he promised and he placed his hand on Hank's shoulder as a gesture of reassurance.

#

Frank visited weekly after being alerted to the crime committed against Julianne, hoping to bring comfort to Hank as he struggled with loneliness and fear. Several weeks after the incident, a few days after he called Emma, Frank found Hank sitting in a dark room all alone. The silence there was penetrating; it made a loud racket in Hank's confused brain.

Frank left himself in after no one came to answer the door.

"Any word from her," Frank asked gently, hoping to break the spell that held his friend in bondage.

"No!" Hank shook his head slowly and sounded angry.

"I'm sorry." Frank looked for a seat nearby. There was clutter everywhere. Cartons and empty containers of TV dinners had fallen off the coffee table onto the floor and remained there, soiling the carpet.

"When was the last time you ate something?" Frank wondered out loud.

Hank remained silent, motionless. He was numb, cold-eyed and distant.

"The police are looking for him, you know," he finally spoke. "Sheriff tells me he never came home that night. They don't know where he went."

"Don't worry, Bart will come up for air," Frank asserted. "They'll get him."

"Old Joe Mansfield, Bart's father, says he likely left the state," Hank informed. "Heck, could have even joined up with the army. Then again, maybe he went to Canada."

Frank made no response to the notion.

"Hope he gets his head blasted off in 'Nam," Hank moaned. "Deserves it for what he did to my Julie."

"Is she any better?" Frank hoped for something positive but felt remorseful in his asking.

"Can't say so," Hank answered matter-of-factly. "They won't tell me anything," he continued, "don't know what they're doing to her down there. I can't even see her," his voice raised in anger. "Say she needs to be isolated for her treatment to work."

Frank was speechless.

"I don't believe them," Hank groaned.

"Any luck with the other doctor, the private one?"

"It's another dead-end." Hank shifted in his chair and began glaring at his visitor. "That man wants $1,500 up front!" he exclaimed, "calls it a retainer. Will most likely cost thousands more before she is better," he elaborated. "Guess she'd stay in a home of sorts," he paused, "supposed to be pretty posh, though. Good care."

Frank remained silent.

"Where am I supposed to get that kind of money?" Hank demanded with fire in his eyes and then quieted down after seeing sadness come across his neighbor's face.

There was no answer to the question and silence remained for a long moment.

"Has Vincent been here?" Frank finally asked after a reprieve from the bad news. "He wants to know what happened to her. He's demanding answers," he warned. "He might come here to talk to you."

"I think he was here," Hank admitted. "Someone was pounding on the back door and hollering. I think he was here more than once. But I didn't let him in."

150

"I'll tell him not to bother you anymore," Frank suggested reluctantly

"Well, the kid might have a right to know," Hank softened momentarily, "But I don't see how it helps Julie," he said resuming his posture of anger. "She was a little sweet on him, you know," he acknowledged. "I don't think she would want him to know about it."

"Guess I can see your point," Frank admitted.

"I, we," he corrected himself, "have to do everything we can to protect her from any more hurt," he paused, "Even bad news."

Frank nodded in agreement.

"Promise me that you won't tell Vince," Hank demanded, to Frank's surprise. "I don't want anyone to know where she is," he noted. "The more people know, the harder it will be for her," he continued, "after she gets out."

Frank was beginning to feel uncomfortable with the conversation. He didn't want to compromise his promise of truthfulness to his grandson. And, it would be unpleasant relating this visit to Emma when he returned home. He reached for his hat. "Guess I should be going..."

"I swore your wife to secrecy," Hank reported. "Now you must promise!"

"Yes, okay," Frank agreed reluctantly.

Hank left go of a long sigh that pushed some stale air, foul smelling as it was, toward his guest.

"We're praying for her," Frank said as he stood.

"Yeah, lot of good that is doing," Hank moaned, still not caring if his words were offensive to his friend.

"Don't give up on God," Frank said in warning as much as encouragement. "Stay put," he finished, "I'll see myself out."

Later that evening Frank asked Emma the question that was pressing on him. "What do we tell Vince?"

"What can we tell him?" she answered his question with one of her own. "That she was taken to the hospital. We aren't told how she is doing. She can and likely will contact him when she wants to."

"But he wants to know why and what happened," Frank continued.

"That's it. That's all we can say. He can't know that we are choosing Hank over him," she reasoned. "Besides, it is for his own good."

#

A few days later it was Earl James who pressed repeatedly on the intercom button. He was becoming impatient with Susan's delay, or refusal to answer.

"Mister James, did you call," she finally acknowledged his summons.

"Where is Miss Culp?" he demanded. "She is late for her appointment with me."

"Gone," the receptionist replied with a single word intended to hit him hard.

"What do you mean?"

"Released about an hour ago," she lifted her finger off the button and chuckled to herself. "Didn't they tell you?" she said as a smear.

"Explain yourself," he demanded. "Who released her, and why? How did this happen?"

152

"Into the hands of the renowned Doctor Chamberlin," she answered in a tone that was schmuck.

The intercom clicked and she listened intently for another moment. Then the indicator light went out, as he spoke not another word. She laughed to herself and opened her desk drawer to reach for a candy bar. This event deserved to be celebrated.

#

Julianne was saved in the nick of time. But how?

CHAPTER SIXTEEN

"After I ran back to the house, you know, the night we met, that was when Bart abducted me. He was crazy, mad with jealousy. I think it was him that saw us."

As Julianne continued with her account of past events, Vincent wondered what Barton may have truly been capable of.

#

Sunday, July 13, 1968 – it was the fateful day for Julianne Culp. It was after midnight when she sneaked out of the house, excited to meet Vincent at their secret place. Little did they know; Bart was prowling about the place.

She had returned to her bedroom and was finally drifting off. It was about 1:30 AM when Bart stepped slowly, softly, as he advanced toward the living room window. A dim light was flickering there.

Hank, uncomfortable with all that ailed him, had taken a sleeping aid that evening. He fell asleep in front of the television set. The local broadcasting company was signing off with the playing of the National Anthem. The music and loud static noise didn't arouse him as he snored loudly.

Peering through the glass window, Bart could clearly see Julianne's father sleeping there. Through an inside doorway he could also see the front foyer and the staircase. Beyond it was the kitchen area and the rear door. He quickly decided to use the rear entrance, keeping initial entry sounds away from the slumbering man who resembled a giant as he reclined there.

The rear porch groaned under his weight as he carefully closed the spring-loaded screen door. Without such restraint, it would slap loudly at its jambs.

In stealth mode he glided through the kitchen under Hank's radar. A few steps creaked but the old man was not aroused. In the upstairs hallway he saw two doors with another at the end. He went to the second one, tightly closed, with a beam of dim light spilling upon the carpeted floor through a crack underneath it. With a half turn of the doorknob it

154

opened to reveal a girl's room, obviously so, identifiable by the colors and accessories.

Julianne was there, her red hair tossed upon the pillow, her body covered by a single sheet printed with a flower pattern. An evil grin of anticipation came upon Bart's face as he took a step forward. He reached to his right side to retrieve the bowie knife, a long broad blade he used for hunting and carried in a sheath there. The moonlight streaming into her room through an open window reflected upon it, casting a bright spot upon the wall above her head.

Her bed had frills on the bottom and a canopy on top. Her sheets were satin. She wore an oversize pajama top that was buttoned down the front, similar to a man's cotton dress shirt.

From a few feet away, he lunged at her and held his hand firmly over her mouth. She squirmed under the pressure of the intrusion and opened her eyes. They became larger as she recognized the intruder. She attempted to free herself of his grip, but he restrained her as he pressed down on her head.

"Quiet!" he ordered and flashed the knife in front of her face, its tip resting upon her nose. "I don't want to cut you, but I will, if you make me," he warned.

She squirmed and slid backwards, pushing herself upward into a sitting position, which he allowed; all the while she watched the knife he waved in front of her face with terror displayed there.

"I saw what you were doing with our little boy Vinny," he admitted. "If you're good enough for him," he paused and rephrased, "well let's just say I want what he got and a whole lot more."

He gagged her and tied the cloth snugly behind her head. Then he took her wrists, placed them together and wrapped a rope around them tightly, leaving a lead of several feet.

"Come on, we're going for a little walk," he snarled through an evil grin.

Julianne's muffled screams were highlighted by the fire in her eyes. She threw her feet off the mattress and kicked at his crotch but missed her target as he dodged the strike.

Holding the rope lead with one hand he retrieved the knife with the other and swiped at the air in front of her. While striking at an invisible target his ears turned bright red, the color caused by the anger that exploded within him.

"Listen, my pretty," he scolded and squeezed her chin hard enough to contort the form of her mouth. "If you can put out for him, you can put out for me too," he smirked and paused, "I know what I'm up for," he warned. "With kidnapping and rape being my crimes, this can only end one way - my way."

She pulled away and screamed but the muffled sounds failed to penetrate through the walls. She wondered where her father was as tears filled her eyes.

"Don't try anything," he warned, "or I'll slit the old man's throat." His eyes narrowed with hatred as he said it and continued, "Then you can watch him bleed out like a pig and die in the pool of his own blood."

Julianne began to cry and shake her head.

"Then you'll cooperate?" he asked, and she quickly nodded affirmatively. There were more muffled sounds as she spoke words that only she heard in her mind.

"I'll go with you. Just don't hurt my dad," she attempted.

He led her through the rear yard and up the trail that led to the strawberry field and packing shed. She pulled back on the rope and yelled through the gag. He led her past the farm and into the woods. It seemed like more than a mile that he continued to yank on the rope and threaten her as they went deep into the forest and then up a steep hill. She saw an outcropping of rock along the ridge.

It was a large overhang, a place referred to as the Indian Cave, which Bart had prepared for his fornication. The cave was fortified with tree limbs and leaves to form a wall in front. Inside his den he built a fire ring and stacked fuel, broken branches, nearby.

There was no talking between them now. She fully understood his intention and cried softly, her sobs shaking at her shoulders.

"Sit down," he ordered.

She looked down at broken rocks and small pools of mud that formed the floor, wondering where to lower herself.

"I said to sit down!" he repeated and pushed her backwards.

"I'm going to make us a fire," he offered. "It will be nice and cozy," he suggested.

When he released the rope and turned his back to light the match, Julianne saw her chance to escape. But as she turned to run he lunged at her and grabbed her ankle. She spiraled downward, striking her head on a large rock.

She laid there motionless; her eyes were closed. Blood was pooling under her head.

Assuming her dead, Barton had his way with her as she remained unconscious. "Too bad," he said looking down on her exposed body, her clothes torn away. "At least it wasn't all a total waste."

He lit the fire and lingered there, considering his plight and plotting his next move. He watched her intently and considered the urge to rough handle her once again, but began to feel sympathy for the girl he wanted, rightfully at first, but then allowed lust to reign as it commanded him to fulfill his every desire.

An hour went by and she didn't move.

Bart fled the scene under the cover of night before the break of dawn.

CHAPTER SEVENTEEN

"They were searching for Bart. You know, he disappeared the same time I did. I had no idea what happened to him; then the letters began to come," Julianne explained. "They were from Bart, and at first, I refused to open them."

"He pleaded for forgiveness. He claimed meeting God in the rice fields of Vietnam after watching his buddies die there." Her eyes glossed over and tears swelled.

But Vincent's expression remained hard, cold. He felt no sympathy for Barton, and little for Julianne. He had been left in the dark, like a

158

soldier captured and thrown into the dungeon. The doom and gloom of that place still lingered in his heart.

#

The recruiting office was located in a small row of nondescript shops, dirty and unkempt, resulting from the unfulfilled promise of developing a thriving business community. The large poster hanging in the window displayed a soldier in full gear holding a walkie-talkie. Behind him a row of others walked through a water filled trench, bearing their arms. "Be No. 1" it enticed, "Your future, your decision… choose ARMY."

Next to it was the customary Uncle Sam poster with him pointing and declaring, "I Want You for U.S. Army."

"Can I help you?" a good looking uniformed young man glanced up from his huge gray desk.

"I'm trying to identify this boy," Hank answered. "We got a letter from him. Can you tell me where he is?"

"I hope so," the officer answered.

"His name is Barton Mansfield," Hank continued. "We inquired back in July," he continued, "but he couldn't be located then. Now we got a letter," and he displayed the envelope.

"May I see it?"

Hank made no objection and offered it to the recruiting officer.

"It's been stamped by his APO and that should indicate its origin," he noted.

"APO?" Hank asked.

159

"Oh, sorry," the other man paused, "that's the Army Post Office from where it was mailed."

"I see," Hank said, "and what is your name," he paused, "if I may be so bold as to ask?"

"But of course," he answered, stood and extended his hand. "Jeffes, Sergeant First Class, ROTC, stationed in Fort Indiantown Gap. William Jeffes… at your service," and he produced a broad smile.

"Nice to know you," Hank said, his response seemed lackluster following the enthusiastic introduction of the sergeant.

Returning to his office chair, he again focused on the envelope. Then he stood and walked to a large file cabinet. He walked his fingers through the long stack of papers held in a large folder and eventually pulled one out. After examining it for several minutes, he spoke softly. "You said Mansfield," and paused, "with an M?"

"That's right," Hank answered quickly, feeling anxiety beginning to rise.

"Don't see him here," Jeffes explained.

"But he's got to be there," Hank suggested in earnest. "You see his letter."

"Sorry." And then he looked at the paper some more. "We do have a Barton Nansfeld," he offered reluctantly. "That's Nansfeld, with an N," he elaborated, "but the same first name."

"That's got to be him!" Hank nearly shouted.

"Could it be?" Jeffes was thinking out loud, "a misspelling?"

"It's him! Got to be him!" Julianne's father sounded suddenly joyful.

"Well, it would have been his place, his responsibility," Jeffes corrected, "to correct a misspelling of his name."

160

The conversation paused as both considered the possibilities.

"Could he have done this intentionally?" Jeffes asked himself. And Hank nodded.

"Do you know him? Can you identify him in a photo?"

"Absolutely!" Hank confirmed. "Know the boy well," he lamented, "too well."

"Wait here," Jeffes ordered and went into a back room. A few minutes later he returned with three folders in his hand. Carefully he opened each one, removed the photo attached to the front page with a paper clip, and then placed them on his desk, facing outward for Hank to view.

"Do you recognize anyone?" Jeffes asked.

Hank looked closely at the young men displayed there in dress uniform, standing in front of their flag, the stars and stripes boldly displayed in the background.

"That's him," Hank tapped on the center photo with his forefinger. "That's Barton Mansfield."

"A misspelling," Jeffes acknowledged, "now isn't that something," he suggested. "I'll have to look into this further."

"Do you have any contact information on this enlisted man," he paused, "this Mansfield? Perhaps you know his address, or next of kin?" Jeffes asked as he handed a blank paper to Hank.

"I'll give you what I know," Hank agreed.

"So, you have this letter," the recruiter noted, "what is your interest in Mansfield?"

Hank stiffened as his eyes glossed. "He's wanted by the law!" he shouted. "Kidnapped and raped my daughter."

"Now wait a minute," Jeffes blustered. "That is a serious accusation," he paused, "why isn't the sheriff involved?"

"He is," Hank fired back. "Police are looking for him. Like I said, we asked for him here in July."

"Do you have any proof of this? Do you have any papers?" Jeffes paused, "a warrant, or… maybe a police report?"

"Not on me, not now, but I can get them. That's not a problem."

"We'll need the papers from the proper authorities."

"Yeah, sure," Hank agreed. "But where is Bart now?"

"He's fighting for his country. He's in 'Nam. In the thick of it."

Hank waited for more information.

"Have the police department contact us," Jeffes instructed. "In the meantime, I'll check into this misspelling issue." He began to retrieve the photos placed on the desk. "That has to be settled and corrected first."

"He's got to pay for his crimes," Hank demanded. "He can't just run off, join the Army, hide with them, and get away with it."

"I agree with you," the officer was now feeling the heat. "But there is procedure. Proper procedure. He's fighting with the U.S. Army in a foreign country. He's not living the easy life," Jeffes countered. "These things take time," he warned. "Once his identity is confirmed, then the charges are established, extrication papers will be filed with the Army. It's going to be some time before he returns back home to face his accusers."

"I'll be back," Hank said with a huff. "Start your paperwork. You're going to get a lot more." And he turned to leave.

#

It was extremely hot that day and the air was so thick that he could cut it with his knife. They were walking along an open road headed toward a secluded village where insurgents were said to be hiding.

Suddenly there was rapid gun fire. Before Barton could drop to the ground the boy from Kentucky, a second earlier walking alongside him and chatting about his girlfriend, fell into his arms. As he watched the boy's life slowly ebb away, his heart burst open and tears pent up by a lifetime of hate were released like the waters that rage through the floodgate, violently crashing into a meandering stream. Barton's sobbing drenched the face of his fallen comrade, washing away the grime that smeared the face of the suddenly deceased.

A lieutenant grabbed his collar and pulled him away as bullets sprayed nearby, thumping upon the earth with a flare of dust. They ducked behind an armored personnel carrier and survived the onslaught of enemy fire.

His unit regrouped and it was a week later that they were ordered to counterattack.

In formation the helicopters swooped in, swaying from side to side, like a swarm of bees -angry hornets going after the intruder of their hive. A Huey Cobra led the assault.

Behind the village of huts with thatched roofs exploded an inferno of flames, almost touching the tails of the A-4 Skyhawk bombers as they raced ahead of the bursting bombs they just released.

People were running in every direction, as if they were ants from a hill poked by the giant's stick. In this horrific scene they somehow did not seem to be much more significant than insects.

The soldiers, privates and sergeants, felt a rush of adrenaline, like the effect of a powerful drug released in their veins. Perhaps they were addicted to the thrill of the attack, even while looking straight into the face of death.

Bullets were flying everywhere as they shot recklessly at those scampering below. The shooters grimaced and hollered profanities, their eyes bulging, their faces wet with beads of sweat sticking there. The collars of their shirts were soaked. The hot humid air blowing through the chopper burned at their faces; they were singed by the fires of hell.

After touching the earth near the edge of the village, Bart jumped out of the helicopter with his comrades of arms and screamed as he ran with them in pursuit of a Vietcong unit retreating into the dense jungle.

He never heard the shot that penetrated his heart. It was fired by a sniper hidden among thick palms. Barton Mansfield fell instantly; face first, into the mud.

Others heard the single shot and quickly returned fire. A small Vietnamese man dropped from his perch, his body banging against tree limbs as he fell to the ground.

A letter, already sealed and addressed to Julianne, was in Bart's vest pocket, waiting to be mailed to her. The bullet that killed him penetrated the note. Blood poured out of his chest wound, staining the envelope. This was his third letter written to her, and it would later prove to be the most significant.

Julianne had received letters for many weeks but at first ignored them. She hated the memory of the villain, a man she despised, but could not bring herself to burn them either. After some time, nagged by

164

curiosity and guilt, she finally opened the first envelope that was delivered. Barton was sorry, sincerely apologetic.

In his first letter he apologized and pleaded for reconciliation. She was stunned at his request.

In his second letter he feared retribution, punishment for his sins. He claimed to have found God in the midst of the insect infested rice paddies of South Vietnam. Words of forgiveness were spoken by the chaplain, the man Bart sought out after his best friend was killed in action. But absolution was not to be attained there. Bart needed to have her forgiveness.

At the description and expression of remorseful contrition, Julianne was suddenly gripped by his attempt at penance and although still not willing to forgive, she sensed his need. She knew that she would later regret it, but she decided to write back to her assailant. He needed to know of her trauma, what he caused, so that he could be held accountable. He had, after all, left her for dead.

Reluctantly, intending to cause even more guilt, she informed him that he had caused her to conceive. It was a brutal, inhuman act that she could not bring herself to reference in the usual way, indicative of relationships that bonded people together with lasting commitment: family, a father, his daughter.

By the time he sat down to pen his third letter, Barton had received her reply. He was notified of Julianne's pregnancy. The news caused him to be greatly distressed.

He was in the tent barracks writing another letter to Julianne when the siren sounded and he quickly folded and placed it in an addressed envelope and then into his vest pocket.

When Julianne received his reply, a hole in it was evidence of the bullet that struck his heart. It was soaked through with his blood, streaking much of the ink he penned there, only hours before his death.

Julie was horrified at the sight of it. She thought to quickly discard the note, but then wondered what could have been so important, why someone went out of their way to make sure the letter was delivered.

She clearly saw the words, "…can't be mine…" and on the next line were scrawled the letters, "…I didn't have sex with you… and even if I did, it is evident that I am infertile. Shooting blanks."

She was not ignorant of the irony of the message and her hands trembled before dropping the paper.

In his final letter, Barton denied the possibility of being the father of her child. Was it a cruel haunt; perhaps a final act purposed at tormenting her some more, or even worse, for implicating Vincent? Her mind swooned.

But what was the secret they kept?

#

Julianne told her daughter, Brianna, that her father died in Vietnam, and gave him a fictitious name. Barton's body never did return from the battlefield and his remains have not been accounted for – ultimately, he is MIA.

CHAPTER EIGHTEEN

"After I received that last letter from Bart with his confession, I had to reconsider. I relived it all. Most of the memories are painful, with the exception of the two of us."

And Vincent wondered what might have been.

"He wasn't the only male I was with that night," she cautioned while raising her eyebrows. "You know, we went further than we intended to."

Vincent rolled his eyes.

"Bart claimed that he couldn't be the father…"

#

Vincent sat erect in his bed as he watched the alarm clock sitting on the nightstand. The ten o'clock hour was dragging on. Its minute hand seemed to be reluctant as it reached for the quarter past mark on the clock's face, the number three. The young man was anxious about his impending meeting with his girlfriend and released a long sigh, blown between his lips. It couldn't come soon enough.

He reached for a comic book and began to examine its pictures.

Then his head bobbed and suddenly he was jarred back awake, his forehead wet in a cold sweat. The vision he had just encountered was still clear in his memory bank and he wondered at the meaning of the nightmare that repeated in his subconscious mind once again.

A giant mechanical monster was making grinding noises beneath his bed. It rattled and puffed out huge clouds of black smoke. Recognition came slowly until he understood its purpose. It intended to suffocate him; this he knew. It was the lung machine.

Just then Nurse Jill saw his distress and came running to save him. She sat in her usual place, the chair by his side, but looked away as she yelled for help. Then, upon returning her gaze, she had changed. Now she had the familiar face of Jewel. She smiled intently, even eerily, as she seemed to be waiting for his impending death. A little dog barked as it pranced on the floor.

Then he saw a Guardian hovering nearby, transparent like a ghost. At that moment Vincent was apparently returned to his bedroom as he recognized the closet on the rear wall. The door suddenly sprung open and other phantoms, other Guardians, burst forth from the darkness there, rushing at him in a horde, then suddenly flapping their wings as they transformed into flying animals that looked like giant bats, their fangs still dripping with blood.

11:30 P.M. Vincent refocused. He had nearly missed his appointment. He shivered briefly as he wiped the sweat off his brow.

12:00 AM, it was the time they agreed to meet for their secret rendezvous. Vincent put on a black, hooded sweatshirt zippered in front with pockets. One of them he filled with a handful of Chocolate Kisses.

He held the screen door until it closed fully and stepped lightly onto the rear porch, choosing the floorboards he knew to be solid. Stepping onto the flagstone walkway he looked to the moon and thought about Julie waiting for him in their secret garden of love under the tall pines. As he darted for the shielding of the hickory tree he noticed his shadow running in front, eerie but not evil, his reflected self leading the way for fulfillment of the passion that consumed him. The backyard was suddenly transformed into a magical scene of suspense and romance.

He quickly traversed the half-mile to Julie's house and ducked behind a tree trunk to examine her home. Like an invader he paused to reconsider his plan, reflecting on his next steps. He would circle around the property to find the trail in the rear, the one that led to the upper fields, connected to her backyard. From there he knew the spot, marked by a drainage ditch always soggy with water that seeped from the mossy patch under the thicket of pine trees.

Alongside the house Vince brushed against a briar bush that grabbed his jacket. He paused and tugged at it, then glanced back toward her house. "Com'on, com'on," he mumbled softly and heard a popping noise as he stepped forward. It was a large branch, fallen from a nearby tree the night before, now snapped in two. Vincent froze there, gazed upon the house and just then thought he saw something or someone move.

He stood still and focused some more. His heart was pounding and the vein in his neck throbbed. The base drum was again increasing the pace as his pulse was powered by epinephrine. Vincent squinted, tugged once more, and hearing the sound of fabric ripped, he leaped over the branch and ran for the next large tree. Concealed there he could see Julie's second floor bedroom window. It was open and the drapes hung out. That was the signal. It was a go.

Vincent quickened his pace now, swiftly cutting through the dense air that whistled in his ears as he swayed and hopped to avoid obstacles. He splashed in the ditch as he crossed it and ducked below the low hanging branches. The bed of moss was colored with a hue of violet, enhanced by the moon light, enticing, but vacant still. He wondered if she might be teasing him, momentarily hiding behind a tree. They looked like angry giants in the dim light and offered no greeting.

He dropped to his knees as his heart sank. He just could not believe that she had stood him up. He had seen the twinkle in her eyes and sensed the flutter of her heart as she squeezed his hand that afternoon. After agreeing to meet him she quickly looked to the ground feeling instantly bashful, but when she lifted her head, her face was adorned with a glamorous smile. It was then that she reached for his hand in a gesture of reassurance.

But as Vincent launched back onto his feet to begin his retreat, he heard a splashing sound. Someone was coming. He peered into the dim light and saw her, her figure swaying, her vermilion hair floating on the air and reflecting the moon with a glint of gold.

And another person moved cautiously and slowly along the same trail, a sleuth with a malicious agenda. He crawled with precision as he hunted his prey. He dropped to his chest under a thicket that afforded him a panoramic view of the romantic scene about to be enacted. He steadied himself to control his emotions; the anger that raged inside was like a forest fire burning out of control and scorching the extremity of his facial features.

Vincent reached for his partner as he beamed with joy. "You came," he whispered. "You really came."

"Shush," she responded as she placed her forefinger on his lips. "This will be our secret forever."

Julianne looked long and deep into her suitor's eyes. They were wide with anticipation. The couple kissed and hugged each other tightly. Their eyes met again, shared a smile of approval, and then they giggled as they joined hands and dropped to their knees.

"Wait," Julie almost shouted, still fixed upon his longing gaze. She reached for a backpack dropped nearby, one he had not noticed at first. "Just a second," she attempted to slow the racehorse the boy was jockeying; it was overcome by hormones and fully fired with adrenaline. Julie turned away, tugged at the pack and produced a large velour blanket. Vincent nodded in approval and quickly helped spread it over the mossy patch. Giggling again they lay next to each other. Their eyes, still longing and communicating with unspoken words, asked for permission as they began to explore each other's bodies. Belts were loosened and zippers opened. Each drew in the other and feeling the connection they began to playfully roll back and forth. Vincent felt overwhelmed, like he was losing his mind, but she remained in control, methodical, not intending to go all the way, but wanting still to touch and feel. She pulled on his left thigh to roll him again, now laughing softly and suddenly feeling the fullness of him. It happened. Penetration. Copulation.

Leaves rustled nearby. Julie's body became stiff and then she jerked, pulling away. "Did you hear that?" she demanded. Vincent paused momentarily, looked past her and licked his lips. He drew closer wanting to regain the position just lost. "Vincent, stop! I heard something," she pleaded and began to sit up. Pulling her knees unto her chest, she listened intently. "There it is again," her voice quivered. "I'm sure that I heard something… or someone."

And then, just as quickly as it started, their tryst was over. She pulled herself together jumped to her feet and grabbed at the bag. Vincent was fumbling with his clothes, his hand sticky wet as he gathered himself in. "Julie, wait!" he urged. "It was probably just a critter, something that lives in these woods."

"No! I'm not taking a chance," she demanded. "Vince, I'm sorry," she conceded as she calmed slightly and touched his cheek with the back of her hand. "We'll have another time," she offered, "I promise."

Vincent stumbled as he ran in pursuit. She splashed in the ditch and he felt its spray. On the trail he grabbed at her elbow. "Julie," he pleaded, wanting to use a term of endearment but unable to speak the word. "Please. Please don't panic."

Her eyes hardened and became steely blue. She yanked and pulled herself away, wanting to be free of his grip. "Vincent, let me go!"

As he felt her arm slide out of his hand a cloud covered the moon and sudden darkness overcame him, with gloom crashing in. His ambition thwarted; he sighed as he watched her run to the rear door of her home.

Trailing behind, Barton saw the whole thing. He grinned with evil intent. He decided to retrieve the blanket they left behind and continued to stalk his prey. The night was yet young and still held promise for him. He would wait a few hours and then in the predawn darkness he would initiate his plan, the one so rudely interrupted by his adversary.

CHAPTER NINETEEN

It was one of the nagging questions

that persisted on his mind during his conversation with Julianne. "But the money," Vincent asked, "where did the money come from, for your doctor?"

"Oh, you mean my psychiatrist? After I was suddenly released from the mental hospital I was taken to a private facility, and Doctor Daniels really helped me. Yes, the treatment was expensive and it wasn't until years later that I learned how my father was able to pay for it. That became my pathway to forgiveness and healing," she prequalified the story she was about to tell. "It truly was a miracle, God's intervention," and she paused for effect. "I got some of the information from my father, but eventually I talked with your grandfather, Frank too."

#

It was September and a hurricane was coming up the coastline. No one knew where or if it would make landfall and most predictions had it turning back into the Atlantic.

Dark, heavy clouds rolled with the gale force winds that howled into Sweetened Vales. The residents had battened down the hatches and waited inside for the storm to pass. Everything was packed into his shop and Frank had that door securely locked. The truck that was usually parked under a shed roof that extended off one side of the barn looked vulnerable so Frank moved it at the last minute and left it in an opening. He stood there and examined the trees nearby attempting to determine if the vehicle was beyond their reach. They tipped and swayed as the winds began. The birches were already beginning to spin in a circle.

174

It rained like cats and dogs for more than a week. During a reprieve from the storm's fury, Frank pulled on his rubber boots and hooded jacket and stepped outside to assess the damage. Large tree limbs littered the lawn everywhere. An old spruce had toppled over, falling onto the garage, its root ball extending upward from the ground, leaving a large crater there. The shed roof was torn away, boards and sheets of corrugated aluminum smashed against tree trunks like tinker toys with the thin metal curled to from a wrapping. But the truck seemed to be undamaged, although it was littered with twigs and leaves.

Torrents of water were rushing everywhere. The drainage ditch that extended away from the barn and alongside the driveway was full, overflowing, and ripped away part of the flat surface in front of the garage that was attached to the house. The roadway was submerged under several inches of water as it pooled there in front of his home.

There was damage everywhere and it would be a big cleanup but the main structures were still intact

. Frank was concerned and relieved at the same time. It would be several more days until he would be able to check the top fields where erosion was known to be a potential problem.

God must have hit the off button, knowing they had enough. Quicker than it began, the storm suddenly abated. The iron layered horizon broke apart as if it was hit by the hammer of the great blacksmith. Bright sunlight streamed through the crack in the sky. "Look," Emma called to her husband, "It's a rainbow, the brightest one I have ever seen."

Frank rose from the chair where he was strapping on his boots, moving to look out the window. "It's the sign of God's promise," she said. "All will be well."

It was tedious, slipping and sliding on wet stones while navigating deep puddles and streams of water, but Frank trekked onward, determined to survey his entire farm. A mist floated on a gentle breeze and moistened his face. He blinked to clear his vision as he approached the upper fields. Under a stream his foot found a flat surface and he noticed the support it offered in contrast to the mud that sucked and pulled at his boots. He paused, pushed down and rubbed the surface with the bottom of his foot as he twisted his ankle. It was a metal box, formerly buried, now exposed by the force of erosion that was generated by the storm.

He later learned that the total amount of rainfall they received was more than ten inches.

Curious about his find, He scraped at it some more and the running water began to expose its surface. He found the edge of the box and there was a handle there. The water slurped and spun with a popping noise as the box came out of its hiding place. It looked old. He fumbled with the latch and gasped as he lifted the lid. Gold! It shined in the sunlight. The box was full of old coins; gold coins, $10 and $20 dollar liberty heads, and his arms began to weaken under the weight of its responsibility.

"Holy smokes," he said softly as his mind reeled with thoughts of what to do next. This would pay for all of the needed repairs, or maybe he could finally get the new tractor he wanted and needed for so long.

And then it became clear, he was absolutely sure and without a doubt Frank knew what he would do, must do, at that very moment. He turned back and started for Hank's house. This was the miracle they prayed for and just what his daughter needed. This gift was intended for them and Frank had the joy of being His messenger.

Hank reached in with both hands and lifted the gold coins, letting them spill over. "Like the one I lost," he remembered, "just like my grandfather told me: buried treasure - from the Civil War."

He turned toward Frank. "I can't take these," he stated with firm conviction. "They're yours. You found them on your property."

"It's for Julianne," Frank informed firmly. "Get her out of Haven. Put her in a safe place."

And Hank nodded as his eyes filled with tears. "Thank you, God," he prayed just loud enough for Frank to hear.

"Amen," the farmer joined in a refrain of praise.

"Here, you take one," Hank's hand shook as he reached for his friend. "No, take several," and he picked up some more of the coins in the box. "Keep these. They are reminders… mementos," Hank reasoned.

"Okay," Frank grinned. "Thank you," he rubbed one between his thumb and forefinger. "Thank you very much!"

"No! Oh, my goodness, no! I thank you!" Hank corrected.

And both men, basking in the glitter of gold, the fulfillment of mercy's promise now revealed to them, embraced with a firm hug.

CHAPTER TWENTY

Their final words...

"After all that has happened to me," Julianne paused to reflect on the sentiment, "to us," she corrected, "I felt the need to tell you about my..." (she almost said 'our'), "my daughter."

Vincent's attention was distracted by an artificial sweetener included with the condiments on the table. On the small bottle he saw the words, "Use sparingly," and it further instructed, "a few drops will do it." Its implication was not lost on him as he remembered their romp in the woods.

Then the same question that haunted him for many years returned to suddenly dominate his mind. Vincent felt the rejection of her decision not to contact him during her treatment. Anger stirred within. He needed time to think. He wasn't ready to believe that he could be the father of her child. Surely, Bart was bluffing; manipulating her so that he could be free of any responsibility for the little girl. And now, Julianne wanted to believe that her baby was not the product of a violent act.

"She is such a blessing, undeserved mercy," Julie said of her daughter Brianna, trying to revive their conversation.

"What do you mean?"

"Blessings," she paused and captured his gaze, "they come to us, sometimes unknown, and often unexpected. But what I've learned is that when I become aware of their influence, I must let them fully embrace me."

"Would you like to see pictures?" Holding her wallet she paused to emphasize her point. "When we open our hearts, mercy will pour in."

But Vincent was stuck on the question of why she hadn't contacted him sooner. Why was his daughter, if she was his, denied her birthright to a father? He shuddered at the thought of her now marrying someone else. He felt cheated by her choices.

As he looked away, she saw the pain of what he had become, a young man tormented by the sum of past events, lacking accountability. Rumors stabbed at his heart.

Julianne also knew the regret of secrets kept for so long. Time had changed them, both of them. The smile she had in introducing her daughter was replaced by a frown. Was she guilty of causing such unhappiness in his life?

"Brianna is a good kid," she noted without enthusiasm.

"Julie," he spoke softly to express sincerity. "I never knew what happened, why you and Bart suddenly disappeared. And then, I was told that you were stricken ill, taken to a hospital, but no one would give me any additional information."

"I'm sorry for what happened," he paused, "But I had to move on. You did too." He grimaced as he looked toward a window seeking a greater space to vent his emotions. "You're as good as married. It seems to me that everything is settled."

Julianne frowned and stiffened in her chair.

"So why are you telling me all this now, anyway?" Vincent whined. "You made your choice and you rejected me. You never really gave me a chance." In distrust he thought her intention might be to establish paternity and financial aid for her daughter.

"I," she stumbled on her thoughts. "I'm sorry," she paused, "But I thought you deserved to know."

"Know what?" he almost shouted in reply. "That Barton is a liar?" he demanded. "I already knew that. And I don't know what you expect from me now!"

"I never reached out to you because my father told me Frank said you believed that I enticed Bart," she paused as her eyes welled with tears. "And there was more. That I was easy," she exclaimed as she quickly turned away. Shame came upon her, but she was unwilling to receive its condemnation. "But now… now I believe my dad was lying, trying to keep us apart."

It was manipulation on his part - game theory.

By then rage was ringing in Vincent's ears and he did not really hear her final confession.

"Bart is a liar!" he repeated louder than before. He choked on that final word as he pushed back his chair while coughing, desperately needing air. Suddenly he stood and ran for the exit door.

CHAPTER TWENTY-ONE

Transitioning back to the present.

It was the last time he spoke to her. She did not contact him again. He carried the resentment he felt from that conversation forward for nearly thirty years. Relationally, his was a lifetime of disappointment, hurt, and loss.

His second chance was Roxanne. They met in graduate school. They shared a love of botany and all things nature. They lived together for many years, she became less content with their relationship, and soon expressed a strong desire for children of her own. Vincent married her, somewhat reluctantly, when infertility treatments began. But as a couple, they never did conceive and continued to drift further apart. Their divorce seven years later seemed inevitable. Who had the bad seed? It was never medically determined. Each blamed the other.

Vincent's career as a botanist and plant biologist kept advancing and moving him farther away to larger and faster-paced urban locales. He liked the work atmosphere dominated by a science that demanded fact to resolve theory, putting those suggestions that lacked proof to rest. In his job the gray clearly became black or white with determined perseverance, while the complicated questions of his youth remained unresolved, still grayish.

He often worked in a laboratory adjacent to a greenhouse. His greatest achievement was the altering of the strawberry, making it larger, more attractive, and durable for shipping to worldwide markets. With changes to its genetic composition, it could be grown near the equator, year around, and sold even in countries that remained constantly cold. The new strawberry was, however, denser with a white core that often split in the center, and it was much less sweet to the taste. But the consumer with the "I want it now" mentality didn't seem to mind.

After more than twenty-five years in his field he advanced into phytology, merging the essential nutrients and oils from plants into cosmetics. By this time, he was a loner, becoming increasingly distant from his friends and co-workers, and thinking more and more about his past, dwelling there as he sat alone in a darkened room in his small apartment.

That friend request from Julianne's granddaughter, Celeste Benton, quickly became a catalyst for discontent, taking him to a disturbing unrest about his life. It continued to nag at his mind with increasing intensity.

CHAPTER TWENTY-TWO

Back in the present - Vincent is finally healed.

This day Vincent felt lonely, even isolated, and he wondered if he had brought such unhappiness upon himself. He sighed as he looked at the long list of personal emails unattended and crowding his inbox. He felt rushed and unwilling to spend the next half-hour sorting and answering them. He touched **The Knot** app for quick social media interaction. There were invites to public events, numerous postings by friends on their recent activities, comments on others' comments, etc. and etc. His pages and groups were calling for attention. Among the notifications were new messages, new photos recently posted by friends, status changes, and birthdays. All this demanded his response and he felt overwhelmed before even checking his news feed or market place.

And yet, not a word was spoken. No touch was felt. There was no interaction that included facial expression, voice tone, body language, or any expression that was uniquely and totally human.

It was unlikely that this day he would share a smile, feel a tear, or receive a hug. AI was crowding into his relational life, squelching his emotions.

It was inhuman!

#

The person behind his cubical wall sneezed loudly and Vincent was jarred back to reality. Sitting at his desk he quickly checked work emails and noticed an unusual title among the list. It caught his attention. In bold letters the email asked, **"DO YOU KNOW YOUR OTHER SELF?"**

In the digital age of **The Knot**, a person's cyber image is compiled by AI and constantly updated. It includes much more than one's credit score, debt and payment information.

AI determines their personality type and provides work achievement scores for a rating, a prediction of success. A perspective employer, retailer or provider, accesses the client's profile before determining a price for the item or service they desired.

Likes, dislikes, and comments, as well as other expressions of public opinion made in social media, are all tracked by AI. This too results in additional profiling of the subjected person in relation to their ability to be a team player: compatibility and subordination.

All searches for information on the web are recorded and compiled to determine active interests and the likelihood of a purchase, even estimating the date of such a transaction. AI searches for a bargain, rates products, and alerts the perspective buyer of any relevant consumer review posted on the item of interest.

AI audits all emails and conversations recorded from the person's home and phone.

It knows their complete medical history and physical condition, improvement or decline. It makes assumptions based on determinations from genetic testing, gives consideration to medical records of immediate relatives and even ancestors who are a match, then set goals for nutrition and exercise.

It knew about every event Vincent attended, who he went with, his relationships, even his whereabouts at all times. His preference in music, reading, movies, and YouTube was part of the determinations made for his public profile.

The wisdom of AI's vast intellect is interfaced to prevent any unmerited criticisms, mistaken reports, or hacked data from affecting the creation of the person's cyber being. But this email claimed that recent complaints exposed glitches, potentially relevant flaws in the system, and possibly even sabotage.

Vincent sighed at the thought of persisting through another complicated audit of his *other self.* Unaware of any recent slights, he quickly decided to delete the email, disregarding its warning without further regard. He had more important things pressing on his mind.

As he continued to struggle with intruding memories of Sweetened Vales and the anxious feelings they imposed, Vincent was nearly consumed. He tried to move beyond his past, but so many things in the present triggered those thoughts, musings of his younger days with Julianne and the strange dreams he encountered while heavily medicated in the iron lung.

What was he missing? Surely, there was something about it all that he still had not fully comprehended, or perhaps misunderstood.

He had not yet responded to the nagging request from Celeste, and it appeared daily with other reminders.

\#

This field has long since been abandoned. The farmer who once toiled here has passed. His heirs are busied with the internet.

Theirs is the new age of information, but the half-truths they share are of little value to each other. They are part of the worldwide web, economy and marketplace, and a great cover-up: the hiding of their disappointments, hurts, and fears. Their scars go deep, but AI hides them all. They are represented as happy, always happy and completely content. But isn't it all a vicious lie? Their true feelings have been lost in the false makeover.

Weeds have crept in and now feed upon the fertile soil of this once productive field. What was essential is now disregarded for the desire of electronic illumination, a deafening and dim glow, the lure of perpetual entertainment and appeasement; it will be the cause of their demise.

But there is a sprout here, wild in appearance, spawned from good stock, a surviving root; many decades ago, it flourished in this strawberry field. It was the source of many delicious and nourishing berries.

Still, it offers hope.

A stem reaches upward, stretching toward the sky. A small white flower with soft pedals suddenly appears, awaiting pollination, calling unto heaven. Within a gentle breeze and sprinkling of rain an arch of spectacular color forms.

But unbeholden, this blessing remains unharvested, the potential for genuine kindness and healing. It is waiting still to be bestowed upon its intended benefactor, a victim of disease, a broken heart, or perhaps, one seeking refuge from the curse of the world's travail. But there is no one to pick it, no one to take it to market, and no one to transform it into a therapeutic jam or pie. These were offered with a smile, warm hug, and words of encouragement that brought true healing.

In the twenty-first century it is easier, more convenient and preferred, to get strawberries from the produce section of your local market. They have been genetically altered and are available almost all year around.

And, there is much less caring or sharing among the peoples of earth this day. Many live in isolation. Their connection is only to a device screen, it lacking the touch of a human being. They no longer find joy in simple things, meaningful and beautiful, and most often unexpected: mercy drops. Even the presumption for such is waning, its extinction now nearly complete.

Wind clears the atmosphere. The rainbow dissipates and the strawberry inseminated with blessing remains illuminated, waiting to be discovered once again.

#

It had been many, many years since Vincent's heart bled. His weeping was eventually silenced, becoming nearly unnoticeable, and this came to be his norm. The truth for Vincent was that a beautiful young woman broke his heart and those who should have provided sympathetic understanding withheld it. They offered no explanation; it would have comforted him.

Everyone had their reason, an excuse for their behavior, and a young man killed in a war of attrition conveniently became their scapegoat, their fall guy.

Longevity was a blessing for the original residents of Sweetened Vales. They formed a centenarian's club and had several members in that group simultaneously.

Jerry Kravitz lived the longest, reaching the amazing age of 104, striving another five years after he lost his sweetheart of seventy-two years. Betty went to be with the Lord at the ripe old age of ninety-nine, defying her many doctors' verdicts of terminal illness.

Frank and Emma worked their farm until his seventy-fifth birthday, when he finally announced his retirement. His passing almost twenty years later was a loss acknowledged by the entire community. Emma died a year after that, at the ripe old age of ninety-five.

And Sweetened Vales, (a fictional place characteristic of the real town called "Sweet Valley"), garnered a reputation in its county and state as a wonderful place to live. Having a heritage of healings, the sons and daughters of future generations inadvertently stopped sharing the stories enthusiastically told by their grandparents, and now nearly forgotten, the attention the place deserved and should have received was overlooked.

The small town did not attract the attention of reporters or movie producers who stalked factories in communities said to be plagued by cancer clusters. Sweetened Vales was different. Neither goodness, kindness, or mercy, garnered headlines.

And young families proudly staked their future there as they purchased homes and built new ones, adding several new streets that intersected the old ones distinguished by large shade trees that lined them on both sides.

#

Nowadays, human beings have come to be a pedigree of sort, much like Vincent's genetically altered strawberry: tougher – less tender; not caring about others. We have been changed by time and the evolution of the human experience submerged in new technologies, altered by AI, and now, clearly two-faced.

Yet a person's basic need remains the same. Those who hurt will still seek refuge, and only a touch of compassion will provide their cure.

#

Sitting alone at home, Vincent closed his eyes and just then, as his mind reeled, saw a clear picture from his past. It was Granny Em smiling sweetly. He thought of her as a saint and realized that he should strive to be more like her.

It had seemed that everyone was two-faced, but no... now he could see their striving for kindness.

The memory unveiled settled heavy upon him with an even greater truth. Vincent finally realized the full blessing of his grandparents' earnest love in action. Frank and Emma Vandenberg were kind and caring people. They touched the many lives of those around them. That was, perhaps, Sweetened Vale's greatest secret: the power of kindness to heal.

He smiled to himself at the revelation. And so, he knew that he must choose between privacy and exposure - security and vulnerability; ultimately, it was a choice for denial or acceptance.

Suddenly, Vincent became truly grateful for his heritage, days spent on the farm with his grandparents. This man, the one who witnessed the healings of Sweetened Vales firsthand, felt the past with new appreciation. There was much kindness, generosity, laughter, and love.

Then the scene from yesteryear became dim, replaced by a new vision.

Bright sunlight was streaming into a small room. There were bars in front of him, casting shadows upon his face. The door of his incarceration slowly swung open. The pathway that stretched before him glistened; yellow tiles were interwoven with ribbons of silver. Freedom was waiting for him to take his first step. Regret could hold him no longer.

Julianne was there, holding the key that opened the prison door. Now he must truly pardon her.

Forgiveness was the key for finding freedom from the past: hope for the future.

He heard the promise of mercy speak softly to his heart once again, a calling from the Savior. He answered with acceptance.

And then there was the face of an anxious young woman, possibly a granddaughter. She became visible standing among the shifting shadows. Would he receive her? She awaited his decision.

But she could only be known by a heart that was healed.

With bold anticipation he stepped out of his prison cell. Remorse finally gone; it was replaced with a longing to know love once again. Tears broke loose and streamed down his face. He wiped at them with his shirt sleeve.

#

One should not underestimate the power of prayer. There is healing in sincere, earnest, human expression toward God, even when lacking elegant words or proper sentences. There can be a cloud burst in a sob, a whirlwind in a sigh, an ocean in a tear, a world in a word, heaven or hell in one cry.

With acceptance and forgiveness, Vincent was finally healed. Resentments had been pent-up in him for many years, but he was finally willing to let them go. For in such release there is a simple, but significant beginning, even newness in life.

And so, he went forth seeking that which is true: the fulfillment of blessing another, striving in the service of sacrifice to reap the fruit of kindness and thus propagate the miracle of healing, as others had done before him. He was determined to honor the heritage of those who toiled at Sweetened Vales by giving of himself generously to their descendants, even the family, his family, the one he was about to discover.

So much is different nowadays, yet in reality, everything is the same.

#

He reached into his pocket and retrieved that small orange bottle that contained oxycodone. Knowing that he could no longer expect to find gratification there, he tossed it into the trash. He would not become a statistic in the worst drug epidemic America has ever known.

#

It was a question that had waited a long time to be answered. "Alexandria," he addressed AI to awaken her. "Do I still have that friend request from Celeste Benton?"

"Yes," the voice of the cloud answered, "the request is from 21 days ago. It will be designated to the trash in three more days."

"I will accept the request," Vincent instructed.

"And what is your welcome message?" AI inquired.

"Tell her that we need to talk." he paused, "That I'd like to get to know her," and he hesitated but continued, "That we should meet."

#

Suddenly the light dims as a shadow is cast upon the ground. A large black bird tilts and hovers on the wind, gliding southward for its return to its master's lair. Something is in the villain's beak and it glitters of gold.

EPILOGUE

The Secrets of Sweetened Vales – allegorical:

As a child I was intrigued with my grandfather's farming operation as he raised strawberries on more than fifty acres in Sweet Valley, Pennsylvania. He often irrigated and on a sunny day rainbows appeared. They were beautiful, but not as awesome as the ones that came with storm clouds.

My family celebrated the harvest and yes, I enjoyed, even cherished the many strawberry delicacies described in this book. The large red strawberry, so sweet to the taste buds of the tongue, was anticipated as June rolled around. It was a special treat, during a time that was good. Neighbors really did take care of each other.

And yes, the strawberries grown by Fred Updyke were more delicious than any I have tasted in recent times.

As I looked at the fields and felt the intrigue of the rainbow, I thought of the lessons I learned in Sunday School. God says that He sees the rainbow. At that point we are connected.

Now, many decades later, I know that God truly loves his children and greatly desires to bless them.

Kindness has the power to heal.

For many of us, life is a bumpy road from a place where we were badly hurt to the place where we will eventually experience healing.

We must always say and do the right thing, but insincerity is selfish and makes us two-faced. Social media is training us to be this way, as our communications are expressed through the internet.

AI nullifies passion. Our other self, our profiled self, is portrayed as complete and whole. AI is not yet editing our communications, but that is likely soon to come. Social media must become "politically correct" and AI will accomplish it.

Most often, we don't pursue the solutions needed for our mental, emotional, and spiritual well being. I'm good, you're good, and so we're all good. But worse than that, everything else is right and good. But it's not! It's all a lie!

Without passion, the hurting will not be helped, wrong will not be righted, and evil will not be overcome. Humanity is lost.

Life is a struggle. We must acknowledge our individual shortcomings, seek the help and healing we each truly need, and support others in their striving for the same.

Kindness will heal both the receiver and the giver.

Laugh, cry, love, touch – connect with human passion – live!

Truly, an emoji reaction to a sharing is not enough!

As we love and serve others, God's mood is brightened. He sends another rainbow, glittering exuberance infused with mercy, showers of blessing for the inhabitants of earth. And thus, we find hope; so... may there be strawberry blossoms forever!

Please give us a review: If you find this book insightful, please know that our success depends on your review. CLICK HERE, or go to Amazon.com and search the author's name, "Alan Updyke," or title, **"The Secrets of Sweetened Vales,"** or simply scan this QR Code:

There Shall Be Showers of Blessing

Daniel W. Whittle, 1883

There shall be showers of blessing:
This is the promise of love;
There shall be seasons refreshing,
Sent from the Savior above.

Refrain:

Showers of blessing,
Showers of blessing we need:
Mercy-drops round us are falling,
But for the showers we plead.

There shall be showers of blessing,
Precious reviving again;
Over the hills and the valleys,
Sound of abundance of rain.

Refrain

There shall be showers of blessing;
Send them upon us, O Lord;
Grant to us now a refreshing,
Come, and now honor Thy Word.

Refrain

There shall be showers of blessing:
Oh, that today they might fall,
Now as to God we're confessing,
Now as on Jesus we call!

Refrain

There shall be showers of blessing,
If we but trust and obey;
There shall be seasons refreshing,
If we let God have His way.

Showers of blessing,
Showers of blessing we need:
Mercy-drops round us are falling,
But for the showers we plead.

And God said, "This is the sign of the covenant that I make between me and you and every living creature that is with you, for all future generations: I have set my bow in the cloud, and it shall be a sign of the covenant between me and the earth.

When I bring clouds over the earth and the bow is seen in the clouds, I will remember my covenant that is between me and you and every living creature of all flesh. And the waters shall never again become a flood to destroy all flesh.

When the bow is in the clouds, I will see it and remember the everlasting covenant between God and every living creature of all flesh that is on the earth." Gen. 9:12-16

...how much more will the blood of Christ, who through the eternal Spirit offered himself without blemish to God, purify our conscience from dead works to serve the living God.

Therefore he is the mediator of a new covenant, so that those who are called may receive the promised eternal inheritance,

And just as it is appointed for man to die once, and after that comes judgment, so Christ, having been offered once to bear the sins of many, will appear a second time, not to deal with sin but to save those who are eagerly waiting for him. Heb 9:14, 15, 27, 28

In memory of: Fred N. Updyke, 1908 – 1987

E. Mildred Updyke, 1910 – 1993

UPDYKE BERRY FARM
SWEET VALLEY Strawberries ®

This is the sign that hung proudly on their barn.

Emma Mildred Updyke is seen above with a bountiful harvest.

Fred and Mildred Updyke pose in a packing shed at the end of a busy day.

Sweet Valley strawberries were large and delicious.
These photos were taken in the early 1960's

An early photo at the farm shows pickers in the field.

www.ingramcontent.com/pod-product-compliance
Lightning Source LLC
Chambersburg PA
CBHW032001170626
46807CB00006B/2589